Loonglow

HELEN EISENBACH

WARNER BOOKS

A Warner Communications Company

WARNER BOOKS EDITION

Copyright © 1988 by Helen Eisenbach
All rights reserved.

This Warner Books Edition is published by arrangement with
Farrar Straus Giroux, 19 Union Square West, New York, N.Y. 10003.

Cover design by Jackie Merri Meyer
Cover photo by Franco Accornero

Warner Books, Inc.
666 Fifth Avenue
New York N.Y. 10103

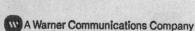 A Warner Communications Company

Printed in the United States of America

First Warner Books Printing: August, 1989

10 9 8 7 6 5 4 3 2 1

Acknowledgments

*I have the most wonderful friends. In particular, I
would like to thank Teresa Cavanaugh, for her
unerring insights and unfailing, ladylike tact;
Eric Ashworth, for his flawless judgment, unflagging
energy, and boundless patience; Carl Ratner, for his
acute mind and the inspiration of his deliriously
pert self; Jonathan Galassi, for his keen, remarkable
attention and wondrous enthusiasm; and
May Eisenbach, for her incomparable example.*

H.E.

Clay had just discovered the truth about man when he noticed the beautiful girl performing a murder.

The truth about man was that he was noblest when supremely intoxicated, and the stunning woman in the booth across from him was breaking someone's heart with the expertise of a hired killer. She had almond-shaped green eyes and used words like "suffocate" and "obsession." The guy she was talking to (Clay couldn't see him, as the booth blocked his view) hadn't made a sound, but the girl went on and on, her voice husky and cynical. She had pale, gleaming skin surrounded by a lush mane of dark curls, but by the time she'd started talking about "psychosis," Clay's loyalties had shifted almost entirely to her victim.

Something prevented him from dismissing her as a heartless killer, though. She might have been doing a job on the guy, but Clay got the feeling she wasn't enjoying it. Her eyes never left her boyfriend's face. Try as he might to hate her, he had to admit the woman was spectacular: tall, slender and exquisitely formed, she had the kind of body he had fantasized about but had never known existed in flesh and blood. A T-shirt and faded jeans showed off her slim waist, flawless breasts and graceful legs as brazenly as if she were dressed in a glittering evening gown. With her face unadorned and shimmering, she could have easily been a former tomboy, the younger sister of a friend who'd blossomed unexpectedly—yet if she'd turned out to be the most exclusive fashion model in New York, Clay would not have been surprised.

Without warning she lowered her voice, laying her hands flat on the table. Clay had to strain to listen; what he heard was crueler than anything he could have imagined. It made her previous words seem gracious by comparison.

She was telling her companion about the time they'd been in love. Her tone was matter-of-fact, almost casual. There was no mistaking what she was telling him: once they'd had it all, and now they'd lost it. She didn't have to accuse him. All she had to do was remind him how things had been. The poor guy must have felt like throwing himself off a bridge because he'd blown it.

Clay felt his throat catch. This was the kind of thing no one should have to hear, not even about someone else. The girl's dead boyfriend didn't make a sound, but Clay wanted to cover his ears and howl. Better that they'd never been in love at all than this. He was drunk, he knew, obliterated, but he couldn't leave, any more than he could stop her. He motioned for another drink and concentrated on blotting out the rest of her words.

Her voice came to a cadence halfway through his fifty-seventh Scotch. She stood, her eyes across the table questioning, as if uncertain whether the corpse would have the ability to revive itself once she had left. "Nothing lasts forever," she said, adding something in a voice so low Clay couldn't catch it. Then she turned and walked out of the restaurant.

Clay held his breath. Would the guy get up and follow? There was no sound or movement from the booth. The cool glass pressed against his hand; the murmurs of conversation in the restaurant seemed muted, somehow far away. Clay was struck with the thought that perhaps he'd imagined the whole thing: what if she'd been talking to herself and there'd been no one sitting with her the whole time? He lurched out of his seat over to her table.

In the corner of the booth, gazing blankly at an untouched hamburger, sat a sandy-haired young woman, as innocent-looking as her friend had been glamorous. She stared up at him with wide blue eyes.

He knew he must look insane, looming over her with his mouth open and eyes bleary from alcohol. "Uh—" he said. "I was—"

She waited to see if he would say more. (It was beyond him, apparently.) After a moment she reached for the check, getting up to leave. "I'm so glad we had this little talk," she said, and slipped past him. The next thing Clay knew, the door to the restaurant was swinging shut behind her.

"How about some action, Emma?"

The first time Clay had seen the beautiful girl, he'd been walking a friend's dog, his third month in Manhattan.

"Let's not take this to extremes," he warned when ten full blocks of hydrants hadn't given Emma inspiration. Passing a sign that promised every kind of bagel conceived by man, he took the dog inside the overheated store; then, coming back out on the street, he saw an unattended pay phone ringing on the corner. He picked it up. "Zabar's," he said cheerfully.

"I'd like to fuck you," mentioned a complex, husky voice.

"Uh, Zabar's," Clay repeated, hanging up before the caller had a chance to get too personal. He glanced up and she came out of Zabar's, without a doubt the most beautiful woman he had ever seen. *Mercy* (he held his breath): dazzling emerald eyes, a dancer's fluid superhuman grace. ("Thanks anyway," he told the ringing phone. "I'm probably not ready for the kind of real commitment you're looking for.") Her arms were graceful, cradling a baguette as if it were a spray of flowers, and when she reached unvarnished fingers up to hook a shock of gleaming hair behind one ear, Clay felt a strange pain in his chest. Right this way, miss, he thought as a flurry of activity swelled the crowd before the store. "Go get her, Emma" (silky ringlets, pale green eyes). So many lovely women graced the streets of New York he'd have thought he'd be immune by now; yet this one defied mortal comprehension.

Abruptly Emma tugged her leash, impatient to examine several items of nouvelle cuisine scattered across the sidewalk. "Must you?" The girl seemed to look right through him as he lurched ahead, twisting to keep her in view. The "Don't Walk" sign began to flash, and she hurried across the street to beat it. Emma chose this moment to go into a crouch.

"What a thoughtful pet you are," Clay observed, watching the girl disappear from sight. He should have just abandoned Emma, raced to take her in his arms; now he would never meet her.

There were times when the whims of New York City reduced him to near-paralyzing frustration. He eyed a woman dressed in rags: did she care that, of the countless women he'd been introduced to since arriving in New York, none of them had affected him as had this anonymous girl he'd never see again? (She did not.) He watched, completely helpless, as the path the girl had taken was obliterated by a stream of people, many of them giving him the coldly approving appraisal he'd grown used to in the past few months. "Something else?" he asked the dog as she prepared to stalk the city once again. "Perhaps you'd like to bite a cop?" A small boy bent to pet her; Emma licked his nose.

Clay thought of his naïve enthusiasm upon arriving from Tennessee, scarcely dampened by the stream of women to whom he'd immediately been displayed as living proof of life on other planets. ("You'd never dream how few real straight men live here," one confided, drifting off before he had a chance to ask what distinguished the truly heterosexual from mere dabblers.) The Futility of Love in the Big City seemed to be a favorite topic in most bars and parties he attended, or at least foremost in the minds of everyone with whom he talked. Yet the explanation seemed obvious to Clay: it was the disconnectedness of New York life, not lack of opportunity, that made everyone feel so isolated.

What a twisted paradise! He loved the city unabashedly. Even now, finding himself perilously on the brink of untoward intimacy with a passerby who turned out to be utterly oblivious to his presence, he could still summon the feeling of elation he'd felt upon first setting foot in Manhattan. New York City: just walking down the street, engulfed by masses of people, was invigorating. Frantic, intense, completely oblivious to even a possibility of the languid gentility he'd been raised to take for granted, the city's alien nature seemed as affectionate as a warm embrace. "Life here is anything you make it," friends said. "No one cares if you act any special way." (Or expects you to acknowledge anyone's existence but your own, he might have added.) He'd never felt such complete freedom; it was exhilarating.

A month went by without his seeing the beautiful girl again. He tried walking by Zabar's around the same time as that first day, but she never reappeared. This is ludicrous, he told himself, but all the same he roamed the neighborhood, trying to retrace paths she might have taken. She never emerged, not from a well-kept brownstone or a cheap hotel. He could always paste signs all down Broadway, he supposed, litter streetlights and bus shelters. (*Lost: woman of dreams, last seen wandering aimlessly with carbohydrates.*) She was probably visiting some girlfriend who was leaving town, he thought, bringing supplies for the obligatory tearful final dinner. No doubt it was her last visit to the neighborhood altogether. She hadn't looked his way once.

Clay's obsession with the girl amazed him. Without his knowing why, her image came into his head as he sat playing piano; unexpectedly, her face would loom those nights he drifted out with friends: going to parties, new clubs, drinking. He'd catch sight of her in crowd after crowd, only to brave a closer look and find a jarring, unfamiliar face where hers had been.

Sometimes it seemed as if a lunatic controlled his actions, goading him to seek the nameless girl although he had no chance of ever finding her. What did other people do? They earned a living, dawn to dusk, then spent the bulk of it each night to blot out the memory of what they'd done all day. It would be so much easier if only he were like his friends: so preoccupied with making money there wasn't time to stop and question what use any of it was.

"What *are* you doing with yourself, white boy?" By the end of Clay's first year in New York, the mindlessness of his days had become so grating he vowed to abstain from any and all social obligations, sequestering himself from everyone he knew. Overwhelmed by the sheer volume of interpersonal contacts the streets imposed, he stayed in his apartment watching the latest political indictment or impending meltdown on the news with increasing detachment, deliberately choosing jazz arrangements just beyond his grasp. There has to be some reason you are on this planet, he told his reflection, though just what it might be remained a mystery. For weeks he grappled with a vague unease, going outside only for specific needs: food, drink, a newspaper.

After two full weeks of isolation, however, the air of his apartment began to seem so suffocating Clay burst from his solitude, taking to the streets as if pursued. The miles passed under his feet without his stopping to consider where he was headed. Finally, as his legs began to tire, he caught sight of a lit sign promising food—and, more important, drink. It seemed a direct invitation, one he could not ignore.

Clay was only on his second drink when he realized what

his problem was: he was suffering his first attack of homesickness since leaving Tennessee. Could that be possible? He celebrated this turn of events as befit a genuine tragedy: with two quick shots of whiskey.

Yet the drinking didn't help. As he consumed more alcohol, memories of his childhood floated through his head unbidden. If he put his mind to it, he could nearly smell his boyhood summers, picture the piercing blue of the sky at sunrise—"a color to which the City of New York has never been introduced," he mentioned to the waitress. (There were so many beauties to which New York had never received even the promise of an introduction, he realized.) Along with these unsettling memories came nagging, unexpected worries about his future, to which he normally gave as little serious consideration as possible. As he began to ponder the path his life would take now that this strange new city was his home, he happened to glance around the bar.

The woman of his dreams, the woman he'd been looking for in vain, was seated mere feet from him, breaking someone's heart. After a few brief moments, the remainder of his evening lay around his feet in a million glittering shards.

The day after Clayton Lee's eighth birthday, his sister Cynthia glanced up from the piano to find him standing in the doorway of the study. "Come here," she called to him. "I want to show you something."

Warily, Clay made his way to the bench. She slid over several inches and patted the hard surface next to her. After a moment's hesitation, he sat down.

"Look"—she placed his hands on the keys—"copy what I do." She played a series of notes, then a chord. He studied her. "Come *on*," she nudged, playing a simple melody. This time his fingers obeyed, faltering slightly. "Close. Try again."

When their father came into the study thirty minutes later, he discovered his son and daughter earnestly harmonizing together at the keyboard.

"What's going on here?"

Clay stopped at his father's voice.

"*Cynthia!*" His father had never used such a tone before on his daughter.

She turned, sighing. "I'm teaching him to play."

At this, Clay's father took hold of Cynthia's arm, pulling

her out of the room before Clay had a chance to find out what she'd done wrong.

That night Cynthia crept into her brother's room when he was sleeping. Clay woke with a start to find her seated on his bed. "What's the matter?"

Her voice was cool. "He didn't come home last night."

Clay sat up, rubbing his eyes. "Who?"

"Daddy." The first time Cynthia had awakened to hear her father returning to their house in the middle of the night, she'd been ten years old; she had lain awake for hours, her blood racing. By the time she was twelve, she'd acquired the ability to awaken, instinctively, seconds before the sound of his even tread on the stairs.

"It's only a matter of time," she went on.

"What is?"

"You'll see."

Clay waited for her to explain herself. "What are you talking about?"

"Mark my words," she answered ominously, then slipped away.

Dulcie Marshall Lee's son had inherited her full head of shimmering fair hair and delicate aristocratic features the years would insolently turn even more attractive than her own. From his father, Clay inherited a tongue capable of devastating unsuspecting targets and a deep appreciation for the curative powers of alcohol. Yet unlike his father, Clay found no need to postpone his pleasures. In no time at all he'd learned which drinks promised maximum effect with minimal evidence of their intake.

Every morning, Clay went swimming with his sister, doing all he could to goad her to rebellion. Afternoons he drank, to brace himself for family dinner; in the evening, he played piano for his mother's pleasure. ("Must you per-

petrate that noise?" demanded Clayton, nearly the first words
Clay recalled his father speaking.)

At seven, Clay realized his father didn't love him as his
mother did, or as Clayton loved his fragile, high-strung
daughter. At fifteen, Clay determined the cause of his father's loathing. His strong physical resemblance to his mother
and his unwillingness to reform a temperament ill-suited to
serious work served as constant reminder of what Clayton
saw as his most ill-fated blunder, marrying the impulsive,
insubstantial Dulcie Marshall. Nor did Clay's undisguised
lack of interest in his father's money help matters (though
Clayton still continued to augment his already considerable
fortune in hopes of influencing him). Money was his father's
chief asset, as charm was his mother's, but Clay cared little
about the rewards of either.

The week after his fifteenth birthday, Clay met Charlene
Watford, one of the richest girls in Tennessee and the daughter
of one of his father's discarded mistresses. Sensing the discomfort such a liaison would cause his father, Clay immediately set about convincing her to be his childhood
sweetheart. By the time he realized Clayton was less dis-
tressed than complacent about the match, however, it was
too late; the course of their affair was irrevocable. Unknown
to Clay, so was the deterioration of his relationship with his
mother.

Charlene Watford was the Watfords' crowning achievement, "no mean feat in a community with as many perfect
teeth as it has millions," the Lees' housekeeper, Mona, had
been quick to note. Charlene's relationship with Clay was
based on little beyond nascent parental dreams of fair-haired
offspring, yet even with a generous dollop of teenage lust,
the romance had no future, for Charlene had a major flaw:
she took life in deadly earnest. When they weren't making
love in or out of doors, Clay tormented her with deadpan

sarcasm, while Charlene analyzed the deeper meaning behind everything he said with a perplexed expression on her face. Clay had goaded Charlene Watford mercilessly, but she'd never caught on.

As the years passed, Clay's mother grew more distant, in tacit disapproval of his breach of loyalty. Dulcie Lee took his retreat into another woman's arms as confirmation that her son had indeed betrayed her to side with his father as she had always feared he would. No longer did he have time to play for or to drink with her. Nor would she allow any resumption of past intimacy when they did find themselves alone together. Once he realized how drastic the situation had become, Clay devoted months to trying to repair the breach, yet she remained aloof, impervious to all his efforts to appease her.

Inevitably, as both Clay and Charlene neared completion of their undergraduate degrees, the Watfords asked their daughter when she planned to marry "that damn boy." Charlene suggested that as Clay was "weird" and "frivolous," they might better turn their attention to waiting for pigs to fly. When Clay learned of this conversation, he called the Watford plantation. Mrs. Watford answered.

"Is it true Charlene says we're through?" Clay asked.

After an uncharacteristic silence, Charlene's mother confirmed that it was, adding that the entire family shared Charlene's opinion of him.

"I am sorry to hear that," Clay said. "There's not another girl in Memphis who likes to fuck as much as Charlene, and I had no idea my tireless efforts were leaving her unsatisfied." He hung up before she had the chance to offer him any sympathy.

When Clay returned full-time to the bosom of his family, he discovered that his father had mellowed toward him so considerably as to assume his son would join him at the legal helm of Lee, Barringham and Sparks. That he had no intention of doing so did nothing to thaw the chill of his mother's now-permanent indifference. All his efforts could not restore his former place in her heart.

Clay began toying with the notion of leaving home and going North, perhaps to New York City, where the preponderance of blacks, Puerto Ricans, and Jews would discomfit both his parents equally. "Child, you are crazy," Mona said as he lay listening to Erroll Garner and dangling his feet off her bed. "What makes you think the world is ready for 'the blond Duke Ellington'?" Before he could seriously explore this possibility, however, or investigate any other potential options open to him, his sister focused all attention on herself with an orgy of ill-chosen pharmaceuticals. As his parents' sanity and already shaky union foundered, Clay had to wonder if poor departed Cynthia had it better than any of them.

Walking unsteadily from the bar, Clay saw that a pre-pubescent youth was holding a girl of indeterminate years at knife point against an attractive building on Columbus Avenue. This conclusion to the evening's festivities seemed somehow fitting.

Clay had never actually seen someone held at knife point. Instinctively he stopped to watch; a dull thudding filled his chest as he braced himself for bloodshed. He searched his mind for some dramatic plan of rescue, but what little control over his mental functions he had managed to retain after discovering the beautiful girl in the restaurant had evidently vanished with her.

The boy, who must have been no more than thirteen, seemed a full-fledged product of the city's harshest influences, and though the girl appeared to be little more than an urban consumer with limited charms, Clay found himself saddened at the sudden tenuousness of her future. "Hey," he heard himself call feebly. The boy glanced over his shoulder with a smirk that reinforced Clay's suspicions about his inability to meet the city's standards of heroism. Then, as both he and the boy caught sight of a police car drawing slowly across Columbus Avenue, the pre-teen took his knife from the girl's throat and bolted around a corner, leaving Clay to face her. With a toss of overly processed hair, she looked Clay up and down and then walked past him without a word. "That's okay," Clay murmured. "Nothing to it."

The remainder of his trip home was uneventful. Reaching his apartment, he unlocked the door with unsteady fingers and staggered onto his bed, yawning and stretching as he listened to the night's telephone messages.

"How's your progress, boy?" The first voice was his uncle's. (Clayton's brother Wynn had given Clay a month to come up with the outline of a project for a grant he'd scrambled up "to motivate the boy." All that held things up was the slight matter of a theme: Clay was no closer to a topic than he'd been six months earlier when Wynn had first told him about the project. Not that the world would end if he forfeited the grant his uncle had arranged, Clay thought; the idea of someone giving him more money than he had already was too ludicrous to consider seriously.)

Wynn was still trying to convince him that the whole thing was symbolic. ". . . just the push you need," the voice droned on, "to do something of value with your life." Clay sighed, stopping the machine before his uncle finished. "Right," he said. "That's probable." That he might be of value to his ever-devoted parents, Wynn, the firm so busy seeing to the rights of famous addicts and deposed dictators on the loose was a winning concept, if one had a penchant for surrealism. He poured himself a modest cocktail and waited for inspiration to strike.

The next thing he knew, his slumber was shattered by the shrill ring of the telephone. The voice of Charlene Watford, who hadn't contacted him since he'd emigrated to New York, made the perfection of his evening complete.

Since Charlene had made no effort to see him when she'd first come to the city, two scant months after his own arrival, Clay had presumed her new life in Manhattan was too streamlined to accommodate a rude intrusion from her past; clearly she wanted all traces of life in the slow lane erased from her résumé. Her decision to relocate to New York had been as unexpected as his father's earlier move to the East Coast branch of the family firm, but he'd hoped Charlene's choice of the most superficially glamorous city she could find was the final indignity he'd be made to suffer. The sound of her voice destroyed his theory.

"I'm calling to invite you to a premiere," she announced. Culture? he thought. (He'd never known Charlene to show an interest in any activity that wasn't best undertaken in the nude.) Of a dance company, she went on to explain, whose choreographer she'd blown before he underwent The Change.

Her voice brought back a rush of memories. Resisting the urge to ask why she felt the need for weird frivolity or what she thought they'd find to say to one another after all these years, Clay murmured, "Day after tomorrow, then." After a brief, intense exchange, he hung up, covering his head with the pillow. This time there were no further interruptions.

Two evenings later Clay discovered Charlene had grown lovelier and, if possible, more humorless than ever. He took her hand at the door to the concert hall, gazing into her earnest eyes. How was he going to get through the performance without snoring conspicuously and ruining all the good will between them? he wondered, following her to their seats. As if in direct challenge, the dancers instantly got under way.

After an interval of numbing (if well-orchestrated) banality, Clay felt his gaze begin to wander from the stage. He shifted in his seat, scanning the rapt faces in the audience. Several minutes passed before he found himself dumbfounded by a seemingly impossible discovery.

Four rows down from them sat the beautiful girl, like a recurring character in some Fellini movie. Was Clay doomed to see the specter of her glowing face wherever he turned? New York was obviously a mere handful of people surrounded by a great many mirrors. For no good reason, his heart began to pound. (What on earth was wrong with him?) To calm himself, he studied Charlene's face. (Would the woman's beauty startle him each time he saw her float by, he wondered, or would the vision begin to pall with overexposure? There had to be some way to render her charmless, some way of breaking the brazen hold she had attained over him.)

"We'll go backstage, of course," Charlene said once the dance fest had trembled to its heartfelt, brave conclusion. Clay glanced across the aisle for one last look. Yet minutes after Charlene reached the proud choreographer, the girl appeared as if on cue. Walking past them, she went over to greet the most striking of the dancers, a flamboyant black man whose every comment seemed to be driving his admirers into frenzies of appreciation. Every few seconds the girl would say something and the dancer's face would register shock, but before Clay could take in the dancer's reply, Charlene and her soul mate would have a new epiphany on art, drowning out all post-modernist conversation.

Then the dancer flung up his hands and shrieked, "Girl, you get the hell out of this room! We don't allow your kind here!" Taking her by the arm, he tried to race her out the door. She drew herself up to her full height, slinging an arm around his shoulder. He seemed to melt. Almost reverentially, he walked her toward the exit, where she kissed him goodbye, full on the mouth. (It was never too late to take up dance, Clay mused.)

Unable to help himself, he stole away from Charlene's ecstasy to join the other group, waiting nonchalantly until the dancer returned. Then, at a convenient lull in the conversation, he casually asked the name of the girl the dancer had walked out of the building.

Not fooled for an instant, the man let Clay sweat out a few long moments of inspection.

Then he spoke. "You must be referring to Mia D'Allesandro." He put a hand over his eyes as if the thought of her exhausted his bones. "The most lethal woman this side of Gomorrah."

Clay thanked him and went back to Charlene, beaming like a fool. She frowned in confusion, but for once it didn't even irritate him. Free, white and twenty-four, he was at last a man with a purpose.

"Help me," called his sister. Clay dove into the water, but the farther out he swam, the farther away she seemed to be. "What's keeping you?" she cried.

Where were his parents? Clay thought, though their absence seemed familiar, even apt. He struggled through the water; still he couldn't reach her.

"I just want someone to save me," came her plea; then, fading, she went under.

Clay woke. His sister's voice rang in his ears, echoing as if she'd only just left his bedroom. He sat up, looking at the clock next to his bed. Every time he thought about his sister's death, all he felt was his utter helplessness to have prevented it. He rose, rubbing his eyes. The night before came back to him, and then his plan.

Research bore out that Mia was a highly successful stock trader on Wall Street and that neither of her parents—an explosive Italian father and an exceedingly refined French mother—lived in the city. Clay was surprised to find how easy it was to get information on her, thanks to the questionable resources of the family firm. On the other hand, the cost had been first a conversation with his uncle and then, far worse, an invitation to the party Clayton Lee was giving for his latest bride pro-tem. Perhaps his father's lair would be a fitting backdrop for his plan, Clay told himself.

At last the day of the party arrived. It was the first time Clay had seen his father since his mother had bid her husband a stone-faced adieu shortly after their daughter's funeral. Clay would have happily forgone the privilege of seeing his father again, but there was no denying that the firm's ease at puncturing the privacy of anyone in business had proved more than handy. By all reports Mia's salary ran to six figures, and while company gossip noted with some bewilderment that she had no steady boyfriends, there was evidence of regular socializing with the other traders, Wynn had informed him. One such enterprising drinking buddy turned out to be someone Clayton had once fleetingly employed, a young man charming enough to talk any red-blooded capitalist into a date that might enrich her roster of useful contacts.

Clay didn't know quite what he was planning to accomplish by assuring Mia's presence at the party, but he could no more alter his behavior than explain it. In preparation for the evening, he and some whiskey watched the end of *Holiday* in the small room his father had set aside for him before learning of his plan to make his way in the big city unassisted. After Cary Grant somersaulted into Hepburn's arms, Clay went downstairs to survey the terrain.

Mia looked breathtaking. It was not hard to locate her in the crowd—something like brushing a hand through a pile of soot to find a diamond. Clay noted with satisfaction that she was trapped in conversation with his Aunt Celia, possibly the only one in the room who wouldn't be rendered speechless by the dress Mia was almost wearing. The skin of her bare shoulders shimmered, incandescent.

". . . a new job, or they'll think you're a slut," his aunt was saying as Clay approached. (From the sound of Celia's voice, she'd been celebrating for some time.)

"I'll bear that in mind," Mia replied dryly. Wild hair cascaded down her back (Clay suppressed a moan). His aunt went on, oblivious, expounding on the varied outlets fear of sexual expression had taken in their family. Clay interceded, steering Celia toward John and Bettina Willington at large.

Mia tried to slip away, but Clay blocked her path, taking her hand. "Hello," he said. "I'm Clayton Lee, the proud new stepson. And you're—"

"Lucky to meet you, I'm sure." She smiled joylessly, slipping her hand from his and staring down into her drink.

"You'll have to be more sincere, or I'll be forced to call the bouncer."

"Why don't you do that," she suggested dully, throwing back her head to swallow a sizable percentage of her drink. This seemed to rouse her. "What's the matter?" she went on. "Afraid the minute your back is turned I'll start going down on the clams?"

"Pardon?" Clay glanced around.

"Silly me," came her sly drawl, "I guess you don't get many brash Italians in the genteel neighborhoods of Tennessee—not even Italians tasteful enough to be part French. But then you already know that, Mr. Lee, the same way you know my name and no doubt my shoe size."

Momentarily speechless, Clay stared into two emerald specters of anger. Who had told her that he'd wanted her to come—Wynn? Her date? "Clay," he managed. She eyed him coldly, slicing a drink off a passing tray and downing it without missing a beat. "How'd you know I had you invited here, Mia?"

"Why'd you want me here"—her voice was steely—"*Clay?*" Her face was only slightly flushed from liquor.

The alcohol he had drunk earlier was starting to affect him, Clay realized. She had succeeded in unnerving him completely; beauty and angry omnipotence were an unsettling combination. None of this, however, was altering the agonizing state of arousal he'd been in since he'd first laid eyes on her in that dress—when he could so clearly have used the blood elsewhere.

The face of the girl she'd abandoned at the restaurant loomed before him for an instant. How could he explain his actions, his desire for this woman now before him? He cast about in vain for some convincing explanation. The words were out of his mouth before he realized it. "I invited you here, Mia," he said, "to learn how you could have done it." The slightly arched eyebrow only sped his inevitable demise. "How you could take the sweetest girl I've ever seen and just break her heart."

He would have given anything not to have said it. All that effort to get her here and now he'd blown it completely. He was an asshole. He was king of assholes. All emotion drained from Mia's face; she stood, a perfect mannequin, staring past him out into the crowd. "Oh, I see," she said distantly. "You're a friend of Louey's." She put her glass down, her voice chillingly polite. "You'll forgive me if I don't stay." Before he could respond, she strode from the apartment, leaving Clay with an open mouth and the certainty that this time he would never meet her again. The banner of her black hair against a flash of glistening white shoulder was the last thing he saw before the door closed behind her.

TWO YEARS LATER

Monday, 5:48, Louey spotted Mia making her way through the crowd on the Seventh Avenue uptown express. She called her name.

Mia kept walking, and Louey called out "Mia!" again, louder, blushing. This time Mia had to have heard her, but she didn't answer, continuing to make her way through to the next car. The other passengers eyed Louey impassively as she hurried to catch up, her face contorted, an advertisement for stupidity and shame. All the same, she forged ahead, entering the next car just as Mia reached the halfway mark ahead of her. Despite the fact that it was both fully lit and air-conditioned, Mia continued through it, sidestepping assorted white-haired women and dark-eyed boys at the peak of their sexual potency.

A little hoarsely Louey said her name again. This time Mia was at the end of the car; she stepped into the next one, closing the door behind her. It seemed to Louey that Mia was moving even faster than before, but Louey followed without thinking. She had bellowed Mia's name in a public place; obviously all rational rules had ceased to apply. She took deep breaths; she took shallow breaths. Why she had not shriveled into a wilted mass of shame by this point was unclear. She seemed to be on some sort of automatic pilot, as on Mia went, wafting through the crowded underground of New York.

The next few cars were dim, their broken doors not quite closed; windows half open, fans stalled and silent: the external equivalent of Louey's stifling, heart-pounding, clammy self. Now she couldn't bring herself to utter a word, and they traveled together in silence through the darkened train.

Without warning, Louey found herself narrowing the distance between them at an alarming rate. They were in the last car, she realized, at the back of the train. Mia was trapped. Pressing herself against the tiny window, Mia seemed to be imagining herself far, far down the tunnel, safe, away from Louey. The back of her head made one last plea for mercy.

Louey stopped just inches from her, inhaling the scent which, long since faded from memory no matter how she'd strained to recall it, now filled her senses. Suddenly shy, she struggled for the perfect thing to say to bring Mia crashing back into her arms.

"This the Number 2?" Someone jostled her, touching her shoulder. Louey turned in panic, realizing that the doors had opened and the train had stopped inside a station. (From the corner of her eye she saw Mia's wild, dark hair, calling to be ravished.)

"I have no idea," Louey said desperately; this was a lie, she knew, if only she could shake herself down for the information. But all she could concentrate on was Mia. She closed her eyes. Mia was wearing a fuzzy short-sleeved sweater Louey had given her, which bared her vulnerable elbows; Louey wanted nothing more than to pull them around her. Mia's skirt was white, snaked on tightly over her hips and slit up the side to bare inexcusably perfect legs. Louey was staring at her now, frozen, inhaling. If she had any sense, she'd bolt. What was she doing here? She reached out her hand to rest it on Mia's shoulder.

Mia turned. A pair of unfamiliar glasses gave Louey's heart a jolt as her eyes pored over a stranger's face. Then the woman beamed at her. Mia. Louey smiled weakly.

"Hey," Mia said. She removed the tiny headphones which a heretofore undiagnosed mental defect had caused Louey to overlook. "How the hell are you, girl?"

"Fine," Louey said, not mentioning that if Mia kept up that grinning Louey was going to have to get off the train. "How have you been?" The roaring in her ears prevented her from absorbing Mia's answer. After all this time, Mia? She felt feverish. Her teeth ached. Where were her knees?

"Well, see you in another twenty," Mia was suddenly saying. Before Louey knew it, Mia was moving through the doors of the train, which (oblivious to Louey's internal combustion) had reached another station and stopped once again. Louey stood frozen as the doors closed behind Mia and the train started with a lurch.

Louey stared at the glazed windows. There was no telling where she was, or if she should have gotten off the train hours ago. She could feel the rest of the car watching her, the obvious victim, forming their own conclusions. Grabbing on to a strap, she waited to see what the next stop would be, hanging on for life.

When Louisa Mercer was six years old, her mother found her sitting among a jumble of torn papers with tears streaming from her eyes. When Meredith asked what was the matter, Louey looked up into her mother's anxious face and announced that she was going to quit drawing forever. Meredith Mercer put a hand on her daughter's heated cheek and soothed the hair off her damp forehead as she told the little girl, "You're going to make us very proud when you grow up to become famous."

"I won't!" exploded Louey. "I'll never draw again! Karen Willoughby's better than I am." Meredith drew back with a suppressed laugh, but her daughter's face was bitter as she explained why there was no point going on with something if she couldn't be the best. No argument could change her mind.

Louey's birth in a quiet Washington suburb so many years after her two brothers had been an unexpected blessing. Several miscarriages had led Meredith and Edward Mercer to give up hope for the little girl they'd wanted, and when Meredith discovered she was pregnant, she was filled with terrible foreboding. Yet her dread changed to elation as the little girl emerged from her body perfectly formed: tiny, scowling, and with a fine trail of sandy hair.

Within a week, Louey had stopped scowling, but she soon proved to be a cheerless baby, waking them at all hours with her cries. Her parents (who had been out of the habit of caring for an infant for quite some time) soon began to wonder if the blessing they'd awaited for so long was not in fact a curse. Edward Mercer caught himself on the verge of nodding off far too many afternoons at his laboratory; his wife began to long for the relative quiet of teaching algebra to adolescents.

At eight months Louisa spoke her first sentence, at a Passover celebration at which the entire family was gathered, Louey at the head of the table in her high chair. The boys were conducting their usual search-and-destroy mission with the floating matzoh balls, and the conversation was so lively that a baby's chirps went unnoticed. Finally, at the first pause in the conversation, Louey cried out in a loud, clear voice, "My turn!" Her family looked at her in amazement as her face dimpled in a grin and she added: "Please?"

As soon as she started speaking, Louey became a buoyant, sunny child. By six, she also displayed a talent for drawing everything around her with remarkable precision. Her parents' aspirations for the place she would have in history did not seem farfetched: such a clever, talented child could not fail to make her mark on the world. She would be the new Picasso, or perhaps merely the first Jewish President.

By the time she was twelve, however, Louey had abandoned a number of fields at which someone else had shown even a trace of superiority. Her mother couldn't understand why it was her child could not continue anything at which she'd been in any way bested; she worried that the serious little girl would lose her former delight at so many of life's pleasures. As Louey grew older, Meredith was careful to avoid placing pressure on her to succeed, but by then it was already too late. If her sons were too cavalier about the paths that lay ahead of them, her daughter could think only of the future she was obliged to transform triumphantly.

Then, the summer she turned fifteen, she made a new friend, and her mother once again saw a glimpse of her former little girl, glowing with rediscovered happiness.

"**Y**our friend is here." Louey's mother knocked on the bathroom door as Louey stepped out of the shower.

"What?" Louey shook the water from her ears and toweled her hair dry.

"Your friend Mia."

Louey stood by the closed door, momentarily confused. Who, she thought, was Mia? The bathroom mirror fogged with steam.

"I thought you'd *never* get here."

The first hot night of summer, fifteen-year-old Louey had been lying, restless, on her bed, trying to keep from bolting like an untamed animal, until a carload of her friends had shown up, claiming that the best solution was a drive-in movie. Louey, coltish, with the savoir-faire of Styrofoam, had happily agreed. Yet for some reason she'd been unable to bear remaining cooped up in the car. Ignoring the derisive comments of her friends, she left the car to wander on her own, walking some distance past the final row to reach a grassy, uncongested area. She climbed a little hill to reach a spot as quiet as the car was rowdy (but not so still as to jangle her nerves), and lay down in the grass. Lighting a purloined cigarette to keep her hands busy, she stared at it, turning it around in her fingers.

"I thought you'd never get here," someone said, "you shameless vixen."

Louey looked up into a pair of dazzling green eyes and the most beautiful face she'd ever seen smiling down at her. God, she swallowed, staring. The girl's hair was so dark and wild she had an urge to plunge her fingers in the midst of it. Startled, she twined her hands together, looking down.

"So what's the meaning of this?" the girl went on. "You wear yourself out, honey?" Sighing: "God, the life you lead."

"Uh, hardly." Louey frowned, bewildered.

"Hardly?" Eyes twinkling, the girl moved close to Louey, making her feel nervous, suddenly, and warm. (Her skin was tingling slightly.) "You know of course the law prohibits leaving any underaged vehicle unattended at a drive-in movie. I can't see what choice I have but to call in the authorities."

"I love those guys," said Louey, "especially their hair-dos . . ."

The girl's face was unreadable as she held her hand out for a drag, and Louey yielded, trying not to smile. The bones of the girl's wrist were delicate, though Louey didn't understand why she was so transfixed by someone simply drawing on a cigarette. Inhaling deeply, the girl flung herself down on the ground, tossing her head back as she exhaled smoke. Jesus, thought Louey, no one looked like that. Her legs reminded Louey of the flanks of a racehorse; the mixture of flesh, muscle and bone confused her. The girl held out the cylinder; Louey managed with some effort not to drop it.

"So?" the girl went on. "Don't you have a desperate but eloquent last plea for leniency?"

"If you're expecting a synopsis of the plot so far," Louey said, sitting up, "I'm afraid I can't help you. I wasn't exactly concentrating on the movie."

"You weren't?" Another grin swept the girl's face and Louey felt her skin grow warm again. "Then how will I know which of the heroes escapes with his virginity intact?" The girl's green cotton shirt clung to a slender waist; the faded jeans fit her long legs like skin.

"You could always buy the book."

"Joyce Carol Oates, right? Or was that *Getting Wasted?*"

"No, no, no," Louey said. "Everyone knows Faulkner wrote *Getting Wasted. We* are watching *Getting Trashed.*"

"No wonder I didn't recognize any of the characters," the girl exclaimed. Louey laughed, then flushed at her response. The girl held out her hand. "I'm Mia."

"Zadora?"

"*Damn*"—softly—"and it's taken me so long to establish my new identity."

"Why would you want to hide a thing like that?"

"You *are* a deep and wise young person." The girl spoke earnestly, leaning toward her. Louey smelled shampoo, as if she had just stepped from the shower, hair still damp. Reaching out, the girl shook Louey's hand, holding on to it an extra moment, lingeringly; it took some effort for Louey to extract her own. What is the matter with me? she wondered, eyeing the blades of grass around her feet. "So," Mia said. "Got one of your own?"

"Pardon?"

"A name. All your own."

"Yes."

"That's all I need to know." Mia put a hand up as if to stop her from disclosure.

Louey laughed. "Louey Mercer," she gave in, "but my friends call me Pops."

"Of whom you have many, I'm sure," said Mia, echoing a line from one of Louey's favorite Katharine Hepburn movies. "But that would get confusing for me—I already have a number of girlfriends with that name. Anyone ever call you Louise?"

"Not and retain their teeth."

"Yeah, who can blame them?" Mia shrugged, casually brushing a curl of hair from Louey's forehead. Then she startled Louey, reaching out to stroke her earlobe, rubbing forefinger and thumb together as if to test the softness of Louey's skin. What? thought Louey, facing two unblinking eyes. Her cheeks were burning. She shook herself and rose, her legs unsteady.

"Well . . ." she started; she was blushing, she discovered. Mia smiled and Louey felt light-headed, almost giddy. "Nice, uh, meeting you." The sentence took more effort than she would have thought. So, it seemed, did making herself leave.

"I don't think I've heard you mention this girl Mia, have I?" Louey's mother asked.

"Uh, no." Louey toweled a patch of steam off the bathroom mirror and peered at her reflection. "I met her at the movies with the gang," she added carefully. Surely she was jumping to conclusions; this couldn't be the same person with whom she'd talked for less than fifteen minutes.

"She says you were supposed to go to a party tonight," came her mother's voice. "Shall I tell her you'll be down in a minute?"

"I was going to do homework tonight." Louey was uncertain as to what the proper response should be under the circumstances. "She never told me she was coming to pick me up."

"Should I tell her you didn't remember the party and that you can't make it tonight, dear?"

Louey wrapped herself in a towel and opened the door. "No," she said; it came out louder than she had intended, and she winced. "I'll come down and tell her so myself in a minute."

Louey's mother went downstairs, leaving Louey to dress

hastily. Was this really true? Had the girl she'd met looked up where she lived and decided suddenly to show up on her doorstep? What a bizarre thing, she thought, appearing at some stranger's house and whisking her away. She shook her damp curls and made her way downstairs.

"Hey, Louey." The girl from the drive-in sat in a reclining chair, talking with Louey's mother as easily as if she'd done so hundreds of times before.

"Hello," Louey said, a slight edge to her voice. "You'll have to excuse the wet hair, but I wasn't planning on going out this evening."

"You'll never live it down if you don't at least put in an appearance." Mia shook her head solemnly. "Everyone at the party will be asking about you all night."

"Mustn't be the subject of undue talk," she answered dryly. Mia grinned (which made it hard to stay annoyed with any real conviction). Before she could ask what Mia was doing in her house, one of her brothers came into the room, glancing at Mia's chair, then doing a double-take.

Louey sighed. "Danny, this is Mia. Mia, my brother Danny."

"Nice to meet you." Danny spoke in a voice several octaves deeper than his normal one.

"Louey's told me a lot about you." Mia shook his hand.

Danny flushed with pleasure. "She has?"

"Tell him that story you liked so much the other day," Louey prompted, raising an eyebrow.

"It'll have to wait until next time," Mia said, rising, "or we're going to be late. You ready, Louey?"

There was no choice, evidently, but surrender. "As I'll ever be," Louey said, and rose to go.

Wednesday morning when Louey got to work there were twenty-six messages on her desk: ten from agents, twelve from authors, and the rest from friends who hadn't reached her the day before at home. She shuffled the pile twice, pulling off her running shoes and sliding the Rolodex toward her. It was 8:58. Perfect. None of the agents would be in until ten at the earliest. She dialed the first agent gleefully, leaving her name after his taped message and crumpling the paper with his name on it. Soon she had a pile of crumpled messages in balls adorning the bottom of her trash can and the knot that had already formed in her stomach upon walking into her office was half the size it had been. Not a single argument, cajoling request for money or hard-sell job: and it wasn't even 9:30.

"Don't ever abandon me like that again," her assistant Kevin warned, poking his head into her office. He wore a short-sleeved shirt with wild green aliens on an orange background, plus an orange tie; his hair was still damp from the shower.

"Great tie," Louey said. "Did you miss me terribly?"

"Terribly, and without a moment's relief. Queen Daisy

was on the warpath the whole day. You couldn't have picked a better day to play Camille."

"Who was playing?"

She smiled at Kevin fondly; he was twenty-one, fresh out of college and smarter than she had any right to expect—smarter than most of the editors, right up to their fearless leader, Daisy. (Not that this was saying much; there wasn't anyone at Regent Books who wasn't smarter than its publisher, messengers included.) Louey knew she was lucky to have an assistant like Kevin: hardworking, brilliant, humble. Most of the male assistants resented the subservient tasks the females generally seemed to take as their due, but Kevin served her as if she were his royal liege. "What was Daisy on the warpath about?" she asked.

"Pick a number. Basically it was because she found some mistakes in the Berkman copy and hit the ceiling, threatening to fire the whole copywriting department."

"Naturally she'd initialed the copy herself, mistakes and all."

"An irrelevant detail, Louey, you just can't get good help these days. So she simply had to throw a few tantrums or it wouldn't seem as if she really had the company's interests at heart."

"Millicent get screamed at?"

Kevin nodded. "It was gruesome. Everyone came out of the cover-art meeting looking like slaughtered sheep, and Millicent was beet-red. Then Daisy followed her into her office."

"No exit."

"And continued where she'd obviously left off. Millicent just sat there and took it."

"She always does. Did all these people really call me yesterday?"

"Damon called four times." Kevin raised his eyebrows at her meaningfully. "The man has difficulty understanding the phrase 'sick in bed.' I should have told him you were dead."

"He got his proofs?"

"I messengered them to him yesterday afternoon, as soon as they came in. He said he doesn't like the typeface."

"He specifically asked for that typeface."

"He also mentioned that he hadn't seen the cover proofs yet—"

"They don't exist yet."

"—and that he hadn't seen the back-cover copy set in type yet—"

"He just called them in Monday."

"—and that he doesn't want the cover to be quote typical soft-core idealized faggot shit unquote."

"He said that? Into your virgin ears?"

"No, wait. Maybe it was 'faggot slime.' "

"I'm the only one allowed to talk to you that way." Louey ripped the paper with Damon's name on it into tiny shreds. "I can see I'm going to have to kill him." Louey sighed. "And what did Rifkin want?"

"She was livid. Said her book's in the stores and why hasn't she seen a copy yet?"

"It's out? Shit. I haven't even seen it. Can you get some copies from sub rights and messenger her a few? And we should express-mail the Stud calendars to Bambi this afternoon."

"Already done. She called yesterday in a snit demanding to speak to you. I told her she'd have them in her twisted little hands by noon today."

"Angel."

"Don't start with me. I had a whole army of people yesterday who took your uncharacteristic absence very badly. Took it all out on me, in fact."

"I'll never get a brain tumor again, I promise."

"Are you feeling better?" He hovered near her with genuine concern.

An ashen taste filled Louey's mouth as she recalled the feeling of waking up the previous day without Mia. Her stomach lurched; they might as well have broken up two days and not two years ago.

"Must be feeling better," she said. "How could I face another day with Daisy if I weren't?"

"Or a day without me?"

"Or a day without you," she agreed, patting him on the shoulder. "Well," she sighed, "I suppose it's time I made some actual phone calls."

"Be brave," Kevin said, leaving her office. "Wake me when it's over."

Tuesday Louey had spent the entire morning in bed, staring at the cracks in her ceiling and replaying the moment when Mia had turned around to face her, that easy, guiltless smile lighting her beautiful features and destroying whatever tenuous hold Louey had on sanity. The past two years she'd obviously been deluding herself; she was never going to get over Mia. Mia had been put on the planet specifically to pluck her from the world of the merely mortal and then let go to watch Louey plummet to the depths of hell. All in a day's work, she supposed; no reason to let a small thing like permanent emotional paralysis get in the way of leading a rich, productive life.

A hot shower would make her feel better, she knew, but she didn't want to feel better. She wanted to stay in bed until someone had to send a squad car to make sure she hadn't been brutally murdered. She wanted Mia to call now that she'd seen her and find her number out of service, for Mia to open the paper and see her picture under a grisly headline. Was that asking so much?

Given the nature of the city, she realized, it was amazing that their paths hadn't crossed before now. (Normally, brushes with her past were limited to those with whom she'd shared 3 a.m. cocktails or a junior high school softball association, it was true.) Still, it was sadly appropriate that the first time she'd seen Mia since being deposited on her nose in the rubble would be on the subway. Just her luck to have such an opportunity for a long, soulful reconciliation.

After the bulk of the day had slipped by, Louey hauled herself out of bed and went to make some tea. On a whim, she added a good helping of the rum she kept for guests. The sting was comforting. A stray memory of the first time she'd ever seen Mia wafted into her head, and she choked on a scalding gulp of her drink. A fit of coughing dissolved into sudden tears.

Pathetic: sobbing into her tea. Who was responsible for this behavior? No one *she* knew. Still, she had an idea when it would stop: when Mia called to tell her that seeing Louey had made her realize she'd been insane to toss aside the best thing life had thrown her way. No doubt she would put Louey on retainer just to be her girlfriend, and Louey could quit her job for good. Louey could see it now: Mia would put on a tiny maid's costume and clean Louey's house every week. She'd beg to do Louey's taxes. Who was Louey to say no?

Pouring another shot, she put on a Billie Holiday album. Billie was such a cheery entertainer, she never failed to provoke hilarity. Perhaps I should take control of my life, she mentioned to Billie. She could always take up smoking, possibly, or learn a few tricks with a syringe. Meanwhile, she had plenty of days and nights to wax nostalgic about Mia before she died of terminal masochism.

Lunch Wednesday (after a plethora of phoning) was with Thornton Gaddes, an agent whose association with every celebrity with teeth bored him—"unutterably," he explained (at some length). He was supposed to be intelligent, but Louey couldn't bring herself to sympathize about his latest stellar obligations, and tried to steer the conversation to business projects. This tactic met with lukewarm success.

The check came to $89.82 at the restaurant of Thornton's choice. Louey's veal had been tasteless, but then she shouldn't have expected otherwise for a paltry $30, she supposed. Along with a mild case of indigestion, she'd acquired the knowledge that Thornton had four authors she wanted to work with, though he wouldn't send her two of them and Random House was trying to come up with a few ideas for the other two. Louey started to suggest topics, then realized Random House didn't need any more bestsellers and held her tongue. She shouldn't have drunk alcohol at lunch, she berated herself; the afternoon was going to be endless and unproductive. Usually she guzzled Virgin Marys, but with Thornton's pancake makeup gleaming across the table at her, she'd needed fortification.

By four-thirty, she'd been complained to by eighty percent of her authors and had given out some uncharacteristically stern edicts along with her customary reassurances. Her willpower was slipping; lately she found herself increasingly unable to reassure her authors, and she'd even come close to hanging up on one of them when he'd interrupted a call from London for the third time.

"I don't have to live like this," she told herself when the catalogue copy for the spring list came around written in Serbo-Croatian. Mia was rich; if Louey had been good, she could have been a kept woman by this time, living off the fat of the D'Allesandro money, happy and overfed. "I don't want to work any more," she wailed, buzzing Kevin.

His cheerful voice over the intercom nearly brought tears to her eyes. "Yes, Louey? Your every whim?"

"I want to be blissfully happy," she moaned.

He paused. "Leave New York," he said at last. "You can't get there from here."

After a long swim at the Y, Louey walked home, stopping to eye some movies in the window of her favorite video store. She had at least six manuscripts to get through before Friday, but there was no arguing with either *The Philadelphia Story* or *Risky Business*. At least this way she wouldn't have time to think about Mia.

Katharine Hepburn had nothing on Mia: not with Mia's smoky-lashed eyes and that full French mouth. Katharine Hepburn barely had breasts, not like Mia's. Louey's heart pounded at the memory of the first time she had seen Mia, at the ripe old age of fifteen. She felt barely more than seven now. It was as if not a single day of the past two years had ever taken place.

Fuck you, she thought as Tom Cruise faced Rebecca De Mornay in an empty train. Fuck you, Mia. She turned off the VCR and took a manuscript with her to bed. Half the pages were single-spaced and the typeface alternated, sometimes every other paragraph. God, Louey groaned. When was she going to stop expecting Mia to walk through the door?

Louey Mercer had two good qualities she drew upon whenever possible: an inability to tolerate injustice and an ability to see the humor in almost every situation. When she started at the bottom rung of a publishing house nearly everyone had warned her against, the first quality caused her considerable difficulty, but the second proved invaluable. A fast, tireless worker, she couldn't help feeling that the people around her had stumbled into such an intensely foolish industry through no fault of their own, just as she had. Her tendency to regard everyone from the company president to the mailroom boy as her accomplices in protracted lunacy soon won her the amiable regard of a sizable percentage of the office.

Louey's mother had difficulty understanding why her daughter had chosen to submerge her talents in a job which promised few rewards, monetary or otherwise, but when her rise as an instrument of others' fame came with precipitous speed, she ceased her protests and congratulated Louey on her decided success. When Louey took a new job as senior editor, her mother sent flowers. (The card read "With love from Keith and Mom," and though Meredith protested that the florist had misread her scrawled "With love and kisses," Louey persisted in teasing her mother about her new illicit liaison with the pre-teen who mowed the family lawn.)

Publishing proved to be surprisingly similar to college life: filled with intelligent, articulate people concerned with books and ideas. Yet while in college Louey the student had been center stage, waiting for the day adulthood granted her complete autonomy, publishing booted her to the wings, giving her a never-ending obligation to the authors whose work she championed.

In several years' time she had acquired both a reputation for outspoken, attentive loyalty to writers and a growing impatience for the very job she had once considered so vital. She still saw books as sacred creations (and herself fortunate to be able to develop and occasionally hone unpolished gems when the shaky temperaments of both her charges and her employers permitted). Yet the business was growing less concerned with writers and more interested in those products most easily reproduced on videocassettes or trans-ferred to T-shirts. And as authors' expectations of creative freedom and support grew sadly remote from practical real-ity, Louey's own patience began to thin radically.

Her personal life provided little relief from her increas-ingly dissatisfying professional one. Since her one love affair had crumbled, she hadn't had the stomach to seek another— not that she would have had the remotest notion of how to go about it. For years, Mia had been such a constant in her life that after the end Louey had wandered around in a daze, scarcely able to do anything but work and cry. In the years that followed, tears came less often, but Mia's absence nevertheless continued to inform her days and nights. It was a mystery to her how anyone survived this. She didn't think it possible to live year in, year out so constantly aware that her life was never again going to be filled with a presence as essential as air; surely, if there were any mercy in the world, one would swiftly perish from emotional starvation.

Yet one day Louey discovered that she was once again elated to walk the streets of the city, thrilled to go to a concert, see a movie, eat good food. Perhaps life would go on; could it really be possible not to be forever paralyzed by a sense of inexplicable failure? In a burst of energy she cut off all her hair; the face that greeted her in subway and sidewalk café windows inspired her to risk more dramatic changes. She *could* live happily, she decided, with new sensitivity to life's complex truths.

She had thought she was truly cured at last. Her pleasure had felt genuine, not merely some brief phase she had been passing through. Her friends even remarked with glee, "You see, you *can* survive a broken heart." Little did she know how one chance meeting on the subway would affect her, sending her into a despondency so severe it rivaled the one that had followed the breakup. Louey saw the period of alleged recovery more clearly now: it had simply refueled her for more intense and prolonged suffering. How could she ever have imagined otherwise?

Well, she had been stripped of foolish expectations early in life, it seemed, before any serious optimism had a chance to set in and do lasting damage. As she looked out her office window to see cabs barrel into unsuspecting fellow travelers, she supposed she should consider herself lucky.

"Never!"

"Come on, you have to."

"No, I can't."

"You tiny, helpless creature." Mia shook her head. "I never should have brought you here."

"All right, I'll try it."

"You don't have to, you know."

"Oh?" Louey laughed. "You expect me to believe that, do you?"

"Well . . ." Mia shrugged. "Far be it from me to make you do anything you secretly don't crave."

"That's rich." Louey motioned to the waiter. They were in a small bar close to Louey's school, furnished in what Mia called "shameless decor." "It's getting late, though."

"These guys probably would let us stay the night."

"Four shots of tequila, please," Louey told the waiter.

"For each of us," Mia added.

"Mia!" Louey hissed; the waiter took their order as if there were nothing odd in their request. "Let's not be too cautious."

"A dirty word. What's wrong with going to extremes?"

"Well . . ." She had to admit everything she'd done to

excess with Mia had turned out wonderfully. "Can we go dancing afterwards?"

"First we'll see if you can walk."

"Big words, coming from a practiced lush. You won't be in any shape, yourself. It'll just be harder for the rest of us to tell the difference."

"You're in sore need of some real-life knockout escapades, sweetcakes."

" 'Sweetcakes'?" Louey raised an eyebrow. "Bitch goddess is more like it."

"Talking tough, eh?" said Mia. "We'll see just how the little lady talks four drinks from now."

Their shots arrived and they dispatched them, giggling helplessly, though after two it seemed to Louey they were slowing down considerably. Some time passed before they found themselves aboard a bus back to their homes.

"He knows you're jailbait," Mia whispered as a paunchy gentleman in polyester eyed them disapprovingly; Louey let out a snort. "Mm," said Mia in her ear. "What a hunk. Think you could land him?"

Louey stifled another burst of laughter. "Challenging, but worth it."

"Never know," Mia murmured. "Some of these guys just pretend to be hard to get." She leaned her head on Louey's shoulder.

Louey smiled. "Is that what college boys are like?"

Mia rarely went into detail about her college life, no matter how much Louey pressed. "Sure, every woman's after him," Mia went on obliquely, "but how many can see how deeply sensitive he is?"

"He's not what college boys are like," Louey gave up. Though they were two scant years apart, sometimes it seemed more like a hundred.

"See what I mean?" Mia sighed. "Just thirteen and you know so much already."

Between Mia's school terms they'd drive out to the beach; Mia lived for racing into the waves, pulling Louey with her. She didn't seem to care how far they went; the trick was to lose all vestiges of control, to scream as loud as possible while crashing water overtook you, drenching you completely.

"I guess this is your version of excitement," Louey muttered.

"Cheaper than robbing a bank." Mia closed her mouth in time to avoid swallowing several gallons of salt water. "More spiritual—and so organic, don't you think?"

"A natural woman." Louey tickled her, then fled before Mia had a chance at retribution.

Often they lay baking for what seemed like hours, pale skin tightening in the sun, though Mia never seemed to burn, just glow like shades of coffee with varying amounts of cream. Louey put lotion on her shoulders. The skin on Mia's back was soft as velvet, hot; it made Louey feel odd to sweep her hands across it, perfect body quiet underneath her fingers. All around them the beach revealed human imperfection; what must it be like to be Mia, polished, perfect flesh and muscle? Mia would grow silent, drowsy, sometimes fall asleep under her hands; then Louey would nod off and wake to trickling water on her face or stomach as Mia towered over her, emerging from the water. "Shiftless as the day is long," said Mia, shaking long, wet hair all over her.

"I was sleeping."

"Tell me why it was I took you from the gutter?" Mia sighed. "I was hoping to make my first million off you by the time you reached sixteen. Why do I make such tenderhearted, dumb investments?"

"I've yielded plenty." Louey covered her eyes. Mia knelt and brushed a wet palm over her stomach, making Louey jump. "You've already saved in entertainment expenses, not to mention upping your class rating."

"A lot you know," Mia grumbled, reaching for more lotion, "high-school trollop. In the eyes of everyone who matters, you have brought me only shame and degradation."

"There, you see?" said Louey, smiling. "Exactly what you wanted."

Louey slept fitfully, the memories pouring over her like brandy on a willing tongue, lye on an open wound. They would walk down the street, the city glowing so brightly in the afternoon sun it was like being let in on a wondrous secret. Mia would slip a hand into hers, lighting her from within. Louey would start some silly complicated story, only to glance over and find Mia helplessly stifling laughter. "I'm trying to *tell* you," she'd say, exasperated, but Mia's shoulders would be shaking and soon it would be hopeless; they'd be laughing so hard they couldn't stop—and at what?

Some nights she dreamt so vividly of Mia that for a second, just before she woke, she was filled with such happiness she thought she might laugh out loud. Then the truth would sink in, agonizing.

Weekends in the park, people would smile at them, and Louey would grin back, elated. How could people she would never know, how could strangers smiling at her, make her so happy? It was as if she were part of some magical universe, filled with souls who dared to show their feelings no matter what the consequences. And at her side was Mia, her bracing accomplice: able to grasp life by the shoulders with both hands, shock delight out of strangers, shake joy from the simplest pleasures.

And the world was filled with other women just like them. Louey remembered when she'd first discovered it: when the most unlikely candidates smiled at them in recognition and delight, Louey nearly stared back in amazement. How lucky she was to be shown this secret, to find people she was bound to everywhere she turned.

I *am* lucky, Louey thought. By the time sleep finally overtook her, she had nearly managed to remember why that was.

Clay rose at nine and put on the suit his latest stepmother had given him as a reward for creating what he suspected was the longest book the world had ever known. In two hours he was going to walk down to the office of the latest publisher his father had cleared of libel and plop 512 manuscript pages on the desk of some thin-lipped editor who chain-smoked and had plenty of untouched gray in his long, stringy hair. His father seemed to feel his friendship with the company's upper management guaranteed acceptance of Clay's work, but Clay suspected only trouble would result from this connection. No editor worth his stripes could bear to have his projects pushed on him by company counsel, that seemed clear.

"Finish the damn thing yet?" He should never have told his uncle he'd started writing; that had been his first mistake. Ever since beginning the project, he'd been hounded weekly by a guardian clearly overwhelmed to see Clay focusing on something concrete. Clay had known better than to reveal his book's subject to his uncle, but obviously he'd been less clear-sighted in taking Wynn's word that he wouldn't mention the project to Clay's father.

"What are you waiting for, my old age, boy?" No sooner

had Clay sat with the fat pile of manuscript pages in front of him, rifling through it with some bewilderment that all of this had come from him, written and rewritten in the space of two years, than the phone rang and his father's aggressively complacent voice barged into his ear. Instantly Clay knew Wynn had betrayed him. A moment later he learned that his father had fulfilled his worst fears and arranged for an appointment with a midtown publisher the very next week.

"So it's all set, then," said his father.

Clay had sat for seven days with the completed manuscript in front of him, unable to form any concrete plans as to his next move. "Wynn," he'd nearly crowed the night his uncle called, "I finished it!" For days he had to stop himself from going back and tampering with what he'd written; the thought that it was actually done was unfathomable, somehow terrifying. Nor had a life of idleness prepared him for the richness and intensity that a week of freedom from work showed him. Now, after two years of inexplicable literary endeavor, he discovered that leisure was no burden but a precious gift, more wonderful than he'd had any reason to expect. That he could walk onto the street in the middle of the afternoon, letting the sun beat down on his face without a single obligation to meet, filled him with an elation that made him nearly dizzy. No wonder people had envied his liberty—he had scarcely understood why before his project had taken it from him.

"Maybe this should be my next topic," he considered: the value of losing one's freedom in order to appreciate its true worth. He could write a play in which children were sent to camp only to find themselves in a nightmare of deprivation. Forced to use their own resources to escape imprisonment, they could ultimately discover that their parents had created the camp as a means to enrich their appreciation of life's most precious gifts. (Then they could kill and eat their parents.) At least his father would have no way of promoting a play; that alone was reason enough to consider the idea.

Clay wondered how long this newfound freedom would have the power to delight him. On the other hand, he might not have it for long. At best, this appointment would mean the beginning of extended servitude to a publisher; more likely, it would be the first in an endless string of discouragements.

As the hour of the interview approached, an unfamiliar feeling of anxiety overtook him. He'd never before been judged by a complete stranger, he realized; what if the man treated him with utter contempt, ripping him to shreds with scorn? Who did Clay think he was—why had he ever thought he could publish a book? The sight of his manuscript suddenly provoked a sensation of acute nausea. Had he wasted two years of his life on a delusion of his own talent, soon to be unveiled as the sham it was? Editors looked at hundreds of books and manuscripts a year, maybe even thousands. What made him think this one would care about what he had to say?

By the time ten-thirty approached, Clay was nearly green with revulsion and fear. If he hadn't been so out of practice drinking he would have taken some alcohol to steady his nerves, but the past two years had been so dry as to lower his once limitless tolerance to that of a baby. He tried to play the piano, with pitiful results. If only he smoked: anything to take his mind off what he was about to learn. He should have thought to go running; now it was too late, unless he wanted to try to postpone the interview. Now *there* was an idea—

The phone rang. Clay picked it up on the first ring, exhaling shakily into the receiver. A relieved voice asked if he was Clayton Lee, and if so, could he possibly reschedule the appointment, as his potential editor had suddenly been called to court? Clay wrote the date and time upon his table, assuring the immensely apologetic voice on the line that it was not the slightest bit inconvenient for him to reschedule; quite the contrary. He suggested canceling the appointment altogether, but the young woman assured him that this was the last thought he should be entertaining.

A moment later, Clay was left listening to a dial tone, once again alone. He hung up, feeling as if an enormous weight had been lifted from his shoulders. Then he went into the bathroom and threw up.

"On the other hand," said Todd (Clay's twelfth or hundredth editor so far), "you might try Bjorn Torovil at Tendon & Leeds. His list is small, but this just might appeal."

Clay rose and shook the young man's hand, his head still spinning. You wouldn't mind, he thought, if I don't follow your suggestion for a year or so? Some months of taking in the cream of publishing had left him slightly dazed; whenever he tried keeping straight which pieces of advice had come from whom, which editor came with which house, he had to stop and lie down. The past few months he'd gotten such conflicting (and equally assured) advice, he'd passed confusion and moved on to numb paralysis.

"Make it better."

That had been the recommendation of the publisher his father had procured for him, though it had taken Clay over an hour to receive it. By the time Clay was ushered into the cavernous office where a tall, beady-eyed man sat (immersed in what seemed to be a terminal telephone conversation), Clay's nerves had settled from anxiety to the beginnings of mild irritation. The man motioned him to sit, barely looking up, then spent the next forty minutes swiveling in his chair and arguing over the telephone. "Fire the asshole," he said twice, glaring at Clay as if he were responsible for the asshole's presence on the planet. "I hear this bullshit every day. Who bought that piece of shit?"

Clay was beginning to wonder if he was up to the honor of being published by such a company when the man uttered an abrupt "Dump it!" and hung up, turning to Clay as if he were a delinquent employee about to be terminated. Clay met his gaze evenly.

"This crap"—the publisher motioned to the pile of Clay's manuscript, which his secretary had placed before him at one point in the conversation. "Make it better. Then we'll talk."

Clay cleared his throat. "Is there anything in particular you'd like to see me do?"

"Fix it, fix it, for Christ sake just do it, I don't have time to tell you how to do your job!" The man fastened a burning eye on Clay. "You're wasting my time."

By all means, Clay thought, unfolding his hands in his lap, let's have none of that. "You have no particular suggestions?" he tried. "Recommendations or . . ." The man's attention was now focused on a memo his secretary had placed in front of him, Clay noticed. He sighed, getting to his feet. "Well, sir," he said, astonished by the brevity of the actual exchange. "Thanks for all your time."

The other man squinted up at Clay as if his tone had been sarcastic. "Shit," he said. "You don't look a thing like your father. Some milkman's bastard, probably."

"That's entirely possible," Clay answered, his eyes widening. "By all means share that theory with my father the next time you have a free moment before sentencing." Resisting additional suggestions that crossed his mind, he left the office in a daze.

"Will you hold for Rick Miner?" Clay was surprised to find himself on the other end of a call from the editor two days later. Miner came on the line, barked someone's name, then took his leave with an economy of grace that left Clay short of breath. He hung up the phone and scrambled to write down the editor's name and number, his head suddenly light on his shoulders.

In no time at all, Clay found himself thrown in the midst of a network of editors who represented every kind of publisher imaginable, each happy to augment the list of future possibilities. First on the list was Rowena Merle, a plain-faced, possibly anemic woman of indeterminate age. Rowena wandered out to greet Clay dreamily and in the hour that followed barely allowed Clay the chance to utter two sentences in succession. "Of course I have so many wonderful authors I don't remotely have time to *edit* them, for heaven's sake," she murmured. "Fortunately, I'm able to give my assistant the opportunity to line edit—it's all I can do to return my *phone* calls most days . . ." This did not come as much of a surprise to Clay, who was not fully convinced that she knew the workings of most of her office furniture, much less the name of any living soul beside herself (including his).

After twenty minutes, Clay surrendered to the rolling waves of speech, waiting for the flow to abate before he tried voicing any thoughts accumulated in the interim. Another forty-five minutes confirmed that even utter silence on his part was not enough to effect such a pause.

The editor Rowena recommended turned out to be a starry-eyed young gentleman with the well-rounded personality of a cartoon character (Brenda Starr, Clay decided). Judd Esterhaus was initially too dazzled by Clay's appearance to keep himself from staring (though, to his credit, he did blush becomingly as if to acknowledge this fact). Yet once he had regained his composure, he began to grill Clay about the personal motivation behind writing the book with a thoroughness Clay imagined would have served him well in the SS. Much as Clay tried to steer him to practical questions, Judd seemed reluctant to discuss any of the particulars of the book itself—what he thought its thesis about love and greatness really meant, or how he saw its chance of publication—refusing to believe that Clay couldn't provide more satisfying information as to how much of the book was based on personal experience, his or that of anyone he knew. "Don't you have some dirt?" he said at one point, piteously.

Judd's choice for him was a less waif-like but equally alarming six-foot-four boy editor whose collection of white teeth and doughy, plump cheeks gave him the appearance of an eight-year-old who'd been subjected to one too many hormone treatments. Clay found the young man's tone of voice so inexplicably intimate he was only able to concentrate on snippets of the editor's dialogue. "Just *entre nous*," the giant said (Clay lost track somewhere in the middle of a rococo discussion about which publishers were sleeping with the same bestselling author).

The next few editors went by in somewhat of a blur. There was a woman named Missy whose appealingly snide assistant mentioned to Clay (just before showing him into the office) that she defined the phrase "editor from the waist down." Shaking Missy's hand, he thought of asking her to spare his tender heart, but she seemed so ill at ease with the basics of human interaction he suspected she had difficulty removing her clothes in total privacy, much less in front of company. Next came a stiff-backed woman who ushered a tearful assistant from her office, patted the bun imprisoning her lusterless dark hair and then brought Clay inside. He seated himself in a chair across from her; yet when she fixed a smile on him, he found himself unable to concentrate on anything but the certainty that she was waiting for the perfect chance to sink her teeth into his flesh. After her came Genie, a tall, anorexic woman who extended a limp, bony hand, looked down to tuck in what appeared to be a boy's undershirt, and then surveyed her spotless office as if attempting to detect an overlooked speck of dust or excess of literature. As Clay spoke about his central theory (". . . we project our deepest fantasies on people we think we love, not realizing that the way they make us feel, that power to do anything, doesn't come from them at all"), she seemed to be absorbed in something other than his words. Only when she stopped to ask him, "Who *is* J. D. Salinger?" did he know for certain she was listening.

Afterwards, in quick succession, came a stream of haughty, indistinguishable young men with ponytails of varying lengths, who all seemed quite intent on proving they were not in publishing but rather on the cutting edge of the new wave, whatever that might be.

As Todd, the last of them, showed him the door, Clay wondered if he might do better on his own. Todd slapped him on the back and slipped a copy of a former showgirl's tips on bran into his hand, then slipped away. He certainly could not do worse.

"Enough," Louey pleaded. "I give. I can't stand any more."

"Weakling," said Mia. They lay on the floor in Mia's living room, giggling until their stomachs ached. "Loonlight in Vermont."

"Loon River."

"Blue Loon. Loon over Miami."

"Loonglow."

"It must have been loonglow," Mia warbled, "that brought me straight to you." She sat up, poking Louey. "Look at you—pitiful young creature."

"While you're so shockingly mature." Louey was weak from laughing. "I feel like someone else's lunch. How can you have brought me to this sorry state?"

"What kind of host would I be if I didn't?"

Louey studied the patterns on Mia's ceiling. "The kind of host you are, of course. Incomparable and tacky."

How had she ever found a friend like Mia? Louey wondered. When she and Mia were together, the rest of the world seemed to disappear; they spent so much time convulsed in laughter she forgot that other people, other worlds existed. Her friends scarcely approved, of course, but Louey didn't care; they couldn't bring her the elation Mia did, or the surprise. It struck her as amazing that she'd stumbled upon her, someone who liked her silliness and sarcasm (both of which her friends did their utmost to overlook). She'd never met anyone so unconcerned with commonplace morality, who got away with doing everything she wanted. Mia went haphazardly through life, through attitudes, philosophies: she was an animal, a force of nature, indulging every appetite with no concern for anyone's approval. It seemed to Louey Mia lived on some much higher plane, the way artists lived, or Europeans, concentrating only on sensation, pleasure.

She was an innocent herself where pleasure was concerned. Bandying racy or suggestive comments came like second nature, but the thought of actually doing something with someone terrified her. Once when a boy had asked if he could kiss her, she had blushed so fiercely she could barely meet his eye. Next to Mia, who no doubt took lovers as cavalierly as men were supposed to, she felt no more than a child, a total infant. Yet though she and Mia discussed nearly everything, she was embarrassed to reveal her inexperience.

"Big day Sunday," Mia said, giving her a nudge.

"Yeah, I'm almost legal." Louey bent her knees and swung them back and forth against each other, keeping her feet planted on the floor.

"Old bag. Any major plans for the day?"

"Well, I was going to build an atomic reactor, but if you have something you'd rather do, I can always put it off."

"No, no . . ." Mia shrugged. "Can't top that."

"Family will probably tie me up and force-feed me cake. They usually throw a feeble party with people they think are my friends."

"Must be why they didn't invite me." Mia pretended to be hurt. Louey snorted. "How about spending the day with me?" Mia went on. "I'll even put on clothes."

"The glitter scuba gear?"

66

"You name it."

"What a lucky girl I am," said Louey, sitting up.

"Here she is!" Louey announced at Mia's door that Sunday. "God, the applause is deafening."

"Your birthdayship." Mia bowed her head and let Louey inside. "You seem in half-good spirits."

"And why is that, do you suppose?" She ignored the glee on Mia's face, walking into the house. "How many mortals get a chance to rack up seven decades of pure hell?"

Mia squinted. "You do seem more . . . wrinkled, somehow."

"Thank you," Louey said. In the living room, a bottle of champagne waited. "For me? And here I didn't get you anything."

"I don't know how you made it until noon without a cocktail."

"What's keeping you, then, girlie? Wing it here." Louey plopped down on the couch.

"Women today"—Mia shook her head—"so—ladylike." She popped the cork and filled two glasses.

Louey began to drink, but Mia stopped her, giving a stern look. "To a twisted piece of work," she toasted. "Long may you wave."

"Ditto." A little embarrassed by the attention, Louey took a sip. Mia deposited herself on the couch next to her, curling her bare feet under her. Champagne on an empty stomach made Louey light-headed, and she leaned back, surprised to find that Mia's outstretched arm was resting on the couch behind her. She took another sip. The warmth of Mia's arm behind her was oddly comforting.

After a long pause, Mia rose to pour them more champagne.

"Trying to get me drunk, wench?" Louey said, but Mia didn't answer, sitting down. Louey drank, wondering why her words hung in the air. "So," she said at last, "where are the parents?"

"Ditched 'em. Sent 'em on a cruise around the world."

Louey laughed and Mia jumped up as if she'd just remembered something. "What?" prodded Louey.

"Cake!" said Mia, going to the kitchen. A minute later she came back, a mass of birthday cake cupped in her hands. "There's cake!"

"I see that," Louey noted. "Make that piece yourself?"

"Of course I did," said Mia, shoving the bulk of the confection into Louey's mouth before she had a chance to protest.

"Thanks so much," she sputtered, laughing. Mia reached to push a piece she'd missed into her mouth and Louey raised her hands in protest, gulping, "Special birthday feeding?" Mia laughed. Louey wiped her face with the back of her hand.

"Here, let me help you with that," Mia interrupted. Before Louey knew what was happening, Mia had bent to lick the crumbs from her mouth. Louey's skin went hot. "That better?"

"Uh—thanks," Louey said; she felt the touch of Mia's tongue as if it were still lapping at her lips. Her mouth felt strange.

Before she knew it, Mia had begun kissing her. Mia's mouth was nibbling at hers, teasing her lips apart; she couldn't seem to breathe. Her mouth fell open. Mia slipped her tongue inside, darting and retreating, branding every corner of her mouth. How could Mia be kissing her? "Is this some—?" she started.

"Yes," said Mia softly, looking down at Louey's breasts. Louey's heart was pounding as, without warning, Mia unbuttoned Louey's shirt, pulling it away from her body and slipping her hands inside. Louey started, unable to stop shaking. Fingers stole across her bare skin, making her feel chilled and burning at the same time. Mia kept staring at her breasts, plucking, hardening the tips to points; then Mia pulled her own shirt off and moved in close to brush against her, tantalizing. Louey tried to breathe, to swallow; she was trembling so fiercely she thought Mia would stop and throttle her. She couldn't seem to keep her eyes from closing. "There's more in the kitchen, if you want," Mia murmured in her ear.

"More?" Louey tried to clear her throat.

"More cake," said Mia, skimming lips against her neck, making her shiver.

"Uh, no, that's—" But Mia had fastened her mouth to Louey's, kissing her so deeply Louey was stunned flat against the couch. She tried to move away, to talk to Mia, but Mia's mouth kept coming down on hers, silencing her. Mia's hands stole over her as Mia kissed her almost lazily, breathlessly—and then she was kissing Mia back, her hands were sweeping over burning skin, she was unraveling, nearly faint—how could she be kissing Mia? The champagne must be getting to her. Mia shifted, swaying so the tips of both her breasts teased Louey's again, dizzying, then Mia's hands were at her, stroking lightly, everywhere. "Oh—" Louey exhaled as Mia reached between her legs.

The next week Louey left for her first semester of college.

Sitting in a plush reception area, Clay studied the voluptuous Hispanic woman who manned the phones, keeping out the unwelcome intruders Regent Books seemed to encounter hourly. He gathered from the other visitors that her name, fittingly, was Cookie. The receptionist caught him sneaking a look and shook her head, giving him a bewitching flash of teeth.

"Mr. Lee?" A young man with a defiantly new-wave blond haircut hovered suddenly before him.

"Yes," he said, rising to his feet.

"Thanks for waiting; sorry to keep you. Will you come with me, please?"

Clay was led to a comfortably disheveled office with two outstanding features: a gorgeous view and barely any room to move. How could anybody function in so small a space? he wondered, particularly since every inch seemed to be crammed with books, papers, piles of orange- and green-bound galleys, flagged manuscripts wherever he turned. How could she breathe? And with an utterly breathtaking view, at present gleaming with the sunny weather, how could she do any work at all?

The one thing missing was the editor herself. The young

man apologized again, explaining that she'd been called into an emergency meeting. "But she'll be back before you know what hit you. Would you like some coffee?" Gin, thanks, thought Clay, shaking his head. "Why don't you make yourself comfortable for the next few minutes," the boy added. Why not? No doubt she would be gossiping about her friends or breaking into song before he knew it.

Clay sat down in a chair squeezed into a corner of the office, putting his briefcase on the floor and gazing out the window. Down the hall a man was screaming he would fire the entire staff, they were nothing but a bunch of useless pederasts. And you asked for *useful* ones, thought Clay. Unable to remain still, he rose and went to the overcrowded bookshelves, which housed a remarkable variety of books. His eyes roved over cartoon collections, esoteric literary novels, oversized photography books, novels whose covers displayed women in pearls getting out of limousines, topical nonfiction, books on rock music. Pasted inside the door was a cartoon called "Poodle with a Mohawk" by someone named Lynda Barry, with the caption "You'll never call him Fifi again." This might take some readjustment, he thought; it didn't quite fit the editor he'd had in mind. He opened a cartoon book, laughing at a page entitled "Supermarket Hell."

"Hello?" The door pushed Clay against the shelves precipitously, and a young woman peered anxiously around the corner as he stumbled to regain his footing. "Mr. Lee? I'm sorry—are you all right?"

"Yes," he stammered. "It's my fault, I shouldn't have been—"

"Hiding?" She smiled slightly.

"Trying to steal everything in sight, if you want to know the truth." He was astonished to find someone his own age facing him. "I was hoping you'd take a little longer so I could make off with the bulk of your collection."

"Not that I would have noticed, considering how organized these shelves are." She motioned for him to be seated. "Sorry to have kept you—my employers keep forgetting that *Monday's* the seizure, Wednesday's the full-fledged psychotic break." She sighed, shaking her head. He stared; was she teasing him? She looked familiar somehow, but he couldn't think why. "Thank you for agreeing to meet on such short notice, by the way," she went on, studying him with a puzzled expression, as if she, too, wondered where she had seen him before. "Well," she said finally, extending her hand, "I'm Louisa Mercer, the woman who holds your fate in her cruel hands. Nice to meet you."

"Likewise." He shifted in his seat, examining her face as if it would explain the nagging question in the back of his mind. Her eyes were a clear blue, large and questioning, and her skin was fair and porcelain-fine, radiant as a teenager's. In fact, with a face rosy and untouched by makeup, she looked remarkably like a student. Perhaps it was because she was small that she appeared so young, he thought; he towered over her.

"So"—she smiled up at him. Her smile transformed her face: it was unrestrained, as if she were a gleeful little girl unable to disguise her delight at coming upon him. "You know," she said, frowning abruptly, "you look familiar to me."

"I get the feeling I've met you before, too."

"Must have been the Folies-Bergère," she said, "before you quit, anyway." Her eyes twinkled. This was hardly going as he'd expected. "So tell me about your manuscript."

"Not much to tell." He hated talking about the project; it embarrassed him to hear his voice take on an air of gravity. With her grinning at him, he realized he would rather talk with her about almost anything *but* the book.

As if sensing his reluctance, she changed the subject, firing away questions on a variety of topics and gently mocking his replies. Finally she steered him back to the book.

"Thank you for your note," he said.

"You write a pretty good letter yourself—piqued my curiosity." He flushed. "How'd you get my name?"

"*LMP*," he confessed; the catalogue held names of publishers and editors. "I've met a multitude of editors from personal recommendations, but no one seemed quite right. Finally I decided just to pick a bunch of names and take a shot at writing them. You're the first to answer me."

"Now that's good luck," she teased. "What editors have you met?"

He told her, watching the expression on her face shift from disbelief to barely contained hilarity. At the final name, she sank her face in her hands, her shoulders shaking. "You poor boy," she said, stifling laughter, "you got the grand tour, didn't you? How did you ever manage to single out that group of people?"

He was almost afraid to tell her how it had begun. "Anyway," he added, after a brief synopsis, "I decided I would probably have better luck with someone I picked for myself."

"I'm glad you did," she said. "Now how about a preview? You can tell me, honest."

"Well," he said, "it's called *Flirting with Greatness*."

"Great title."

"Do you think so? I got it from a movie; I was walking downtown one day when I saw this marquee blazing: 'Flirts with Greatness,' quoting *The Village Voice*. Anyway, the book's about—well, you seem like a rational person, but here goes: love and fantasy, the way we transform a fairly basic emotion into this mysterious force, a catalyst that turns another person into someone with almost infinite power over us. In fact, we're responsible for the very emotions we think *they* cause, but instead we glorify the person who provokes these inexplicable feelings in us, relinquishing control. It's not as esoteric as that, really—I've done a lot with movies and music and how popular culture feeds into it, but it's a sort of tribute, if you can believe anyone would want to pay tribute to mass insanity . . ." Seeing the color drain from her face, he trailed off. "Of course, not everyone would consider this to be a legitimate topic for a book," he added.

"No, no, I'm sorry." She shook herself. "You'll have to excuse me, Clay, my mind just lurched somewhere else. I'm in the early stages of senility these days."

"Wait till you see what I say about that." He grinned, patting the manuscript.

"I can imagine. Well, as long as people live and breathe they'll be interested in love and sex. My chief criteria will be your writing and the strength of your perceptions—if they're striking enough to make a reader feel they're new, somehow revolutionary, shedding light on our oldest patterns of behavior. As for my publisher"—she shrugged— "this business likes to put books into categories, unfortunately. A self-help book, for example, has a slot, while a more analytical one like yours may have a hard time finding its niche. It needs to be dazzling, both topical and fun. Not easy."

"The prognosis for my seeing print is getting dimmer by the minute."

She shook her head, leaning toward him. "I don't mean to discourage you. Good writers are always in demand, so if you write well, and you've managed to come up with something intriguing to say, your chances aren't bad. Of course, I think it's a miracle that anything ever gets published, considering how many obstacles a book faces—the number of people who have to approve it, the timing, the climate of the industry toward certain kinds of books, the existing competition—"

"—the connections of the author—"

She nodded, raising an eyebrow. "—the power of the author's family name—"

He clutched his stomach in mock assault.

"—and so many other factors it would make your head spin. If most people knew what publishing was really like, they wouldn't have the remotest desire to go near it." She patted his manuscript emphatically. "But none of that should concern you at the moment. You've got one of the most critical readers on your case"—a quick grin—"and I'll give it my attention as soon as I can, once I've read the twenty-six other rush projects facing me." She brushed away his exclamation. "No, but I will get to it as soon as I can, and I'll give you a call when I've had a chance to read it."

"Could I take you for a drink to thank you? We could always talk about what other careers you think I might be better suited to pursue."

"Brain surgeon," she said. "No need for me to bother reading a line; it's written all over you." He blushed, sheepish, and she held out her hand. "I don't drink, but I will call you with my reaction. Nice to have met you, Clay."

He rose, taking her hand. Towering over her, he found it hard to imagine this tiny woman having such control over his fate. He forgot to release her hand, examining her, and when she pulled away slightly he blushed again, apologizing. "Thank you for all your time, Ms. Mercer."

"Louey. Please. After all, I'll be delving into your innermost fantasies."

"Louey," he said uncertainly. A stray thought prodded his memory. Her phone line lit up and then a moment later flickered expectantly, as if demanding her immediate attention. "I'll look forward to your response," he added, as an insistent buzzer followed and she shrugged apologetically, turning to the phone. Clay made his way out of her office. As he waited for the elevator, her infectious laughter echoed down the hallway.

"Don't boys in New York ever call their mamas?"

Clay's morning started with the cool voice of his mother on his answering machine. "City life must be exciting," she said; Clay opened his eyes. "And call for so much *energy*."

He listened, stretching, then threw off the sheet when she brought up the topic of his moving home as if it were a plan they had discussed. "Hello, Mama," he cut in, picking up the phone. She was silent, tacitly condemning him for his deceit in not stopping the machine as soon as he'd heard her voice. "You woke me up."

"At eight-thirty?" she exclaimed. She always expressed astonishment at waking him, despite the fact that each time she'd called before noon this had proved to be the case. "What were you doing last night to make you so tired?"

"Celebrating, Mama." He waited for her to ask what he'd been celebrating; when she didn't, he forged on anyway. "I finished my book. The one I've been working on for the past two years."

Her voice was guarded. "That's quite an accomplishment, darling. Does this mean you won't be coming home just yet?"

Clay rubbed his eyes. "I've told you, Mom, I live here now."

"Naturally, you're a grown man," she said, "you're an adult now, you don't need your mother. You've got your own money to prove that well enough." As usual this provided Clay with a twinge of guilt; he hated to think of the trust fund to which he now had free access, while his mother was still forced to live off the allotments sporadically dispensed by his father.

"Do you need any money, Mother?"

"Save it for yourself, dear." Her voice grew even more remote. "You'll need all the resources you can muster to find a publisher."

"I've got one looking at it now," Clay said, somewhat sheepishly. Why did telling her such news seem as if it were brutally chipping away at the fragile foundation of her confidence? She should be happy for his success, he thought; instead, it only seemed to emphasize her frailty.

"Oh?" she answered faintly. His stomach lurched.

He barreled ahead despite her, too weary to keep up the delicate maneuvering that conversation with his mother always required. "Yes, Mother. I've been meeting with people. Dad called someone he knew . . . I met an editor yesterday who seemed, uh, smart." There; he'd said it.

A pause followed. "How is your father?" She spoke at last, a note of macabre cheer creeping into her voice. She was on the verge of cracking, he could tell. "And his new— Doris?"

"Deena. They're fine. I've only seen him once, Mom, since I've been here." A random thought prodded his unconscious, then faded. "I've hardly said two words to him in the last three years."

"There's no need to ignore your father for my sake, Clay," she said. Now he could hear the hysterical edge in her voice; she'd begun drinking early. "He loves you, in his way, and he is your father, after all."

LOONGLOW

"And I love you, Mother." Clay sighed. "But I have to
go now. I'll call you soon, okay? Give my love to Mona."

He hung up, feeling as if he'd just done something illegal,
her plaintive goodbye ringing in his ears. Had it really been
years since he'd lived with his mother? It seemed like a scant
weekend since her presence had enveloped him. He could
picture her clearly, her delicate blond beauty set off by a
pastel sundress, a tall cocktail at her side as she reclined in
the sun, fanning herself. She had no one to amuse her these
days, since her daughter and both her men had abandoned
her.

For the first time in two years, Clay rose at nine in the
morning to fix himself a stiff drink.

By the time supper had come—and gone—Clay had worked himself into an old-fashioned alcoholic stupor. He leaned up against the headboard of his bed, staring out onto the darkening street across from him. What gave most people the illusion that life was worth living? he wondered. Money did it for some people; they worked all their lives to accumulate it, and perhaps if they succeeded in amassing great wealth they felt they'd lived up to their dreams. "Strike one," he said; no chance of that for him. There was always love, of course. People did all sorts of things in search of some perfect love, some ideal; for some, its very unattainability was the chief requirement for the true love object. "You should talk," he told his reflection in the darkened window.

Clay lurched out of bed, going to put some music on the stereo. What would have happened, he wondered, if he'd simply drifted on with Charlene Watford, even gotten married? "Droves of bland, blond babies," he thought aloud, shuddering to think how easily such a fate could have befallen him. Bless Charlene's heart for not accepting him as true husband material; who could say if he'd have had the will to put up a struggle against a future with her should she have elected it for them? "Spineless," he muttered. This was the chief feature of his personality so far, it seemed to him.

The sound of Oscar Peterson filled the room and Clay soaked it in, energized by the power of the music. Talent was another ticket to fulfillment: some were born with gifts—musical, artistic, physical—and measured their success by how well they fulfilled their creative potential, acquiring recognition, fame. Clay held his hands out, staring at them. Once he'd been naïve enough to think he had some talent, that was why he had been given music, but that was clearly no more than childish folly. It must be something to be born with a real talent. What must life be like to have Art Tatum's hands, the voice of Ella Fitzgerald, the body of Baryshnikov, the mind of Lily Tomlin?

He didn't fool himself that what he had done by writing a book was an expression of any such gift, just as he had known there was no point in talking of his future as a pianist. "You have no talent"—he sighed—"whatsoever." Unlike his mother, he had never deluded himself that physical attractiveness and a modest ability to charm were the equivalent of accomplishment. If he'd enjoyed writing a book, it had been because the completion of a concrete task was a pleasure to which he was unaccustomed; it was satisfying to see how his mind could work, pairing creative leaps with practical research. He wondered what Louey Mercer would think of the pages he'd written, if she'd tell him he had any ability or anything of merit to say.

On a whim he picked up the phone and dialed her office. It had been three weeks since she'd said she'd look at the manuscript as soon as possible, and though he'd vowed to wait until she called, he had a sudden, overwhelming need to hear her voice, as if by sensing something in her tone he would be given a vital clue as to her ultimate decision. The phone rang and rang. Finally he hung up, glancing at the clock beside the bed. Of course no one had answered, he thought; it was after eight. (Saved from committing a tactical blunder by sheer logistics.) He staggered into the bathroom to examine the effects of his drinking. When he looked in the mirror, the gleaming eyes of a desperate man peered back at him.

Two days later she called him. He returned from grocery shopping to find a message on his machine, her voice cheerful, friendly. No editor was supposed to sound like that, he thought, trying her number without waiting to see if there were other messages on his tape—editors should be subdued professionals, not frisky kids. Shifting from one foot to the other, he waited for her to answer. Just as he was beginning to think about redialing, he heard an abrupt "Hello?"

"Louey Mercer, please?"

"Who's this?" He answered the tense voice and the tone grew instantly warmer. "Oh, Clay, it's Louey, I'm on my other line. Kevin must not be at his desk, or I'd—let me call you back in a few minutes, okay?"

"Sure," he said, momentarily deflated. He hung up, waiting for a few moments for the phone to ring before shaking himself. Get up, asshole, he thought, going to put away the groceries; she didn't have all day just to talk to him, after all.

He had settled down with an Irish coffee when the phone rang. Nerves slightly dulled by the alcohol, he answered, "Yello?"

She laughed into his ear. "Clay? It's Louey Mercer."

"Hi, how are you? Thanks for calling me back."

"I called you first, remember? Listen, I've had a chance to read your manuscript, and I want to talk to you about it."

"Uh—sure, great. When would be a good time to talk?"

"What's wrong with now? Or did I get you in the middle of something?"

"Over the phone?" For some reason the prospect filled him with dread. Five minutes on the phone, dismissing him, and he'd be left with a dial tone? "Can't I buy you a drink while you break it to me gently?"

She resisted, repeating her earlier edict against drinking. I could teach you a thing or two, honey, he thought grimly; he'd never known anyone who seriously felt as she claimed to about alcohol. "I'm sorry," he said after a few moments of trying to persuade her, "this is wasting your time. I just wanted to thank you somehow; of course we should do it during business hours. I can come to the office next week, if you'd prefer."

"Oh, I don't mind meeting you after work; I stay late most nights, anyway." She paused, weighing her options. "Oh, what the hell, let's meet for a drink, why not. It'll do me some good to act like a real editor and expense-account you."

"I won't hear of your treating me," Clay said. "You're doing me the favor—you've already done me a huge favor. When is good for you?"

They made an appointment to meet early the next week, struggling to come up with a place that suited their purposes. Sometimes Manhattan seemed as limited as a small town, Clay thought; it had endless options, but most of them were bad.

Clay hung up the phone with a time, meeting place, and feeling of slightly giddy anticipation. It was going to take some doing to get through the next few days, he realized. He paced the apartment, filled with extraneous energy, picking up the piece of paper on which he'd written the details of their meeting. As if he'd forget. He glanced at the circled location among the scribblings of places they'd both thought of.

One name struck him suddenly. He'd written down but hadn't gotten around to suggesting a restaurant he'd gone to often when he'd first come to the city. He stared at the name, the amazement of his abrupt discovery momentarily stunning him. The barely legible letters loomed large: that was why she was so familiar, he'd seen her there. Years before, when he'd learned the truth about the beautiful girl, the girl he'd gone on to—he covered his eyes. It couldn't be. Of all the people in New York— How could he not have recognized her? How could he not have remembered as soon as he'd laid eyes on her? True, she had short hair now, making her look different, younger—but even so he should have known her instantly.

What were the odds of something like this happening? There was a pressure in his ears, as if he'd been dropped from an extreme height. Would she remember him, too, once she had sat across from him for an entire evening? And what would she do if she did? He hardly knew what to think.

The absurdity of the coincidence made him light-headed. Ah, the twists of contemporary fate, he thought: Louey Mercer. It seemed she had a story of her own. He wondered if he could get her to tell it to him.

By the time Louey arrived, Clay had finished two-thirds of his drink. Normally he didn't mind being kept waiting; one of the things he hadn't understood about New York was why people were always in such a hurry, so frantic to get wherever they were going. What was the rush? Now, however, he could barely sit still as the minutes ticked away. Surely he'd feel better once she gave him her verdict, good or bad.

She appeared at last, seating herself across from him with a faint blush. "Sorry." She was out of breath. "Have you been waiting long?"

"I was early, actually." He wiped uncharacteristically damp hands on his knees. "Never too soon to shatter your illusions, right?" He tried to grin. The waitress interrupted and Louey glanced at Clay, who had downed his drink as soon as she'd finished shaking his hand. "What would you like?"

"Club soda with lemon?"

"We'll have to do something about this self-destructive bingeing of yours." He shook his head. "A club soda, and I'll have another Scotch," he told the waitress. "Do you really not drink at all?"

"Not really. On rare occasions I feel so unlike myself I

do all sorts of things—like drink, or cut off all my hair"—she ran a rueful hand across her head—"but on the whole I'm far too well behaved."

"Don't you ever need to lose control?"

"I guess I'm afraid of what I might do." She shook a finger at him. "I can see where this is leading—you want me to make some sordid confession so you can tell my boss."

Choking on his ice, Clay gulped, "Far from it," swallowing painfully. "So tell me," he managed, "do you like being an editor?"

"Can't help myself," she said. "What other profession lets you plumb the souls of total strangers? Only a small percent of whom turn out to be psychopaths."

"Lucky you."

"You"—she scowled—"are stalling. Listen, Clay, we've got to talk about this thing you've written sometime—and I bet you won't be nearly as alarmed by what I have to say as you seem to fear."

He placed his hands flat on the table. "I'm ready."

"Well, to begin with, you write very well, and I enjoyed reading the book a great deal. No one breathing would deny that we behave the way you say, that this notion of love distorts our entire way of thinking and interacting with people. A lot of your theories are intriguing, and your examples from popular culture are fun, often very witty. I loved the songs you picked, and of course the movie quotes."

"But?"

"Can't even savor a little praise, can you? All of what I've just said is not minor, you know; you've done some terrific work." He took a sip and waited for her to go on. "You're quite a talented writer, lively, clear, original, entertaining." He flushed, amazed to hear the words coming so glibly from her mouth. If only he could make her slow down, say them over, make her stop. "And love is a subject of universal interest—but in decided categories. Now, if you'd written a psychoanalytical book on how to find love— or avoid it—" She smiled briefly. "Or a lighthearted humor book, say the sort of flip treatment that would be ideal with illustrations, or a violently explosive shattering of modern myths to provoke people into changing their lives—*Beyond Love*, say, the ultimate program for giving up those destructive notions that prevent you from fulfilling your creative potential as a person—" She sighed. "You can see how silly it is, trying to tailor a book for an amorphous commercial audience. What you've done, though it does show an enormously popular aspect of human behavior in a new light, is not quite explosive enough, not quite light enough; it's somewhere in between. My fear is that publishers will say 'Who would buy this book?' or 'What would make a person buy it?' Unless you have your own daytime television show—"

"Sorry."

"Or are media-connected enough to raise excitement for the project—"

"I'm not speaking to Phil Donahue until he stops dropping by at all hours, acting goofy, bellowing in Italian . . ."

"This must sound insane to you, particularly since you've worked so hard, with such impressive results."

He couldn't tell her how it felt to hear her say she liked his writing, after all the vague reactions he'd gotten from other editors. "I was terrified the first time I showed the book to someone," he confessed. "I guess I've been afraid to find out I have no talent whatsoever."

"*Clay*. No writer can afford to count on receiving proof of his self-worth from other people. You have to have the confidence to fight for what you think is good."

"I never planned to be a writer. This book is the first thing I've accomplished."

"In your whole life?" she teased.

"Except for passing time." He winced at his words: next he would say his family didn't understand him.

"Curse of the rich?"

"Born laziness," he said, "with a dash of self-contempt I think I got from my mother."

"Your father sounds eager to see you get ahead, from what you told me."

He motioned to the waitress. "I think he felt if he engineered my introduction to publishing, I'd come around to the family firm once I'd officially failed."

She shook her head.

His throat felt dry. "So you think I should give up any dreams of seeing my name in print?"

"Now, I didn't say that. You have a couple of options; it depends on what you'd be willing to do. I can take the book before our board, which would probably mean a less than strong chance for acceptance here. You never know; each case is different. I could also recommend some editors at other houses who might like it."

"More editors?" He clutched his throat.

She toyed with her napkin. "I do think you'd be in for discouragement—lovely rejections, people who like your writing but don't know what to do with your book."

"Any other options?"

"You could rewrite it as a kind of *Cinderella Complex*— give a harsher damnation of living through romantic myth, show how all the greatness we imagine doesn't come from objects of our fantasies but from within. It still won't guarantee you'll get a contract, unfortunately, though your chances would be far better once you did the work. You could set up a program showing what we do that's wrong, how to summon that feeling of transportation without someone else."

"But nobody can do that," Clay said. "At least I've never seen it done. Why else do we keep torturing ourselves with fantasies that make us miserable?"

Draining her drink almost fervently, she put down the glass, her face flushed. "No answers here." Her voice was slightly tremulous; he felt as if he'd deliberately prodded a nerve. "I wasn't serious, by the way." She cleared her throat. "What made you write about this, if you don't mind my asking?"

Later he would berate himself for the alcohol that had caused him to say it. "It was all your fault, actually."

"My fault?" She frowned.

"Shit," he said under his breath. He could still get out of it, he told himself, make some flip comment. Yet when he tried to think of an excuse, his mind was useless, racing blankly to absorb his blunder. The silence stretched on endlessly.

"What I mean is . . ." he tried, but nothing came out. He couldn't believe he'd done this, trapped himself, as if he'd somehow wanted to destroy it, as surely as he'd ruined his chance with Mia two years earlier. Louey studied him, bewildered. Wouldn't she remember that black day herself, eventually, after he began to work with her? Perhaps it wouldn't be so bad, he thought; she had a sense of humor, right? Not quite believing it, he forged ahead. "I had just moved to New York, and I was out drinking, trying to stop feeling like a stranger in a strange land. This was about two years ago. You were—I was eavesdropping on this conversation between a beautiful woman who was breaking up with—I saw Mia, and then you—"

"You know Mia?" It came out hoarse.

"No, well, I tried to—after that day, I sort of went out and got her to—see, that first year, I just couldn't seem to do anything that—I got it into my head that—"

"Clay."

Her tone silenced him. He was looking at an anguished face—and once again he was responsible, as he'd been with Mia. "I'm sorry," he said softly.

"That's why you seemed so familiar." She looked dazed.

"It was—of course I never forgot anything about that day. I don't know how I could have forgotten you." She stared into her glass.

Clay ordered her some vodka; Louey barely noticed when the alcohol was placed in front of her.

"Are you okay?" he said at last.

"Well"—she shrugged. Misery and embarrassment mingled across her face. "I'm afraid this isn't something I can be professional about." She faced the drink and braved a swallow, placing the glass down defiantly. "So," she said. "I guess this isn't quite the publishing experience you had in mind."

"I don't give a shit about that," he said. "The last thing I wanted to do was upset you."

"Did you realize who I was when you asked for this—date?"

"I couldn't figure out why you looked so familiar. It wasn't until after our phone call that I remembered."

"Jesus." She put her face in her hands.

"Ironic that we should meet after all this time—considering the genesis of my book."

"Just think." She smiled bitterly. "You could have chosen so many other variations. A treatise on models turned stockbrokers. Children of mixed parentage and their effect on the economy. And of course the most obvious topic, women who—"

"Louey." He put a hand over hers tentatively and she turned red, picking up her drink without meeting his eye, then downing it. He ordered her another. "I could kick myself for dredging this up for you. Maybe it would be better if I took this project somewhere else."

"My publisher would love to hear the reason that you changed your mind." She drew her hand away. "But that's not why you should see it through with me." She looked at him almost defiantly. "See, I know just the thing to make it work."

*Y*ou might find her heartbreaking, if you cared to bother. You could be sitting across from her at Reggio's wondering how she'd managed to trick you into (all right, no espresso, but how about some—) Earl Grey tea, even a cigarette, when what you should have been doing was being properly West Side, writing letters or practicing piano. You could be exhaling across the table at her as you considered this business of her face. She wears lipstick, you have to admit, an odd, vaguely crimson shade, and her lips are permanently pursed in a Cupid's bow. These are not things you would say about any of your friends—and her hair is thick and wild around her head, coarse to run your fingers through, but always for some reason tempting you to do so. Her heels are spiked, and she wears very tight pants, but the oversized sweaters redeem her: cuddly punk, and it is a good thing you are not having wine (as she is) or you would certainly have to fall in love with her.

At Reggio's she eyes the waiter and mentions that you are dear to her and she loves you. The waiter she calls "my man," making elaborate plans to visit him. You murmur what you think of her into your tea, but she has gone on to discuss the cab driver she had in for coffee, or the rock star

*or bank teller. You call her a slut, laughing, and she tells
you she is "reevaluating this sex thing," as if chances for its
survival are dim. She asks you if you have anything to say
in its defense. You sit your chin in your hand and smile at
her, and she says this will not help; she wants your advice,
and you say as she is the mother of your children you cannot
help but be partial and disqualify yourself from answering.
This amuses her, but she says she is serious about needing
your advice, so you mention that perhaps she has been having
sex with people she does not desire, out of politeness. You
put out your cigarette and discover the inside of your mouth
to be very dry, and imagine kissing her. When she grins at
you, you smile at the waiter.*

*You go to a play and find tears streaming down her face
when the lights come up; this is painful. You crush her to
you. She is still, and warm, and you would like to feel her
moving against you, but she seems to be warning you not
to think about tasting her lips and her skin. You wonder if
you are imagining her resistance. You are certain she must
know you love her, so you make your conversation banal
and reassuring. You feel a little out of key. It is true that
she loves to be told her legs are alarmingly beautiful (this,
too, is painful) or that you are passionately devoted to her;
also true that she will let you play with that shadowy hair
forever even though she claims to dislike being touched this
way. She has told you she loves you. She likes, she says, your
touching her; it is endearing, she says. You know the reticence
you sense cannot be your own, nor can it be imagined, but
you have difficulty accepting this and often push solely to
discover whether, this once, there will be no resistance. You
put out your arm around her, squeeze her shoulder, stroke her
cheek. Sometimes you refuse to touch her to see if she will
touch you. Expecting nothing, you are always surprised—
and somehow a little disappointed—when she does.*

"Sometime I want to talk to you about this femininity

business," she says. "I have a theory that it's almost entirely the voice."

"The voice is a large part of it," you admit. You have explained that several of your friends have an aversion to her because she is such a "girl" (without mentioning, of course, your surprise at feeling no similar aversion). Her voice is endearingly hoarse and girlish, alternating quotes from Sartre and Proust with vulgar, adolescent jokes, yet she likes girlish things: sachets, feathers, ruffles and perfumes (though so did all those Frenchmen).

She exclaims that, if anything, she has always considered herself to be butch. You introduce (gently) the incident when she sprinkled glitter on her stockings and rainbow-painted her face. (Out of pity, you avoid mentioning the accompanying shiny, strapless blue dress.) She protests. You realize she spends much of her time with you blushing and protesting. This must be why you love her. Soon you will start to imitate her, orally underlining words with great enthusiasm, making fascinating swoops of tone and color.

Some evenings she will come over and get you stoned, and you will lie on the floor smiling and accusing her of ruining your self-respect, as you listen to records or fall asleep to the drone of her stories. She will lie with her face next to yours, and the paleness of her skin, her mouth, the perfection of those soft, high breasts, will confuse you. Very slightly, the faint perfume will make you ache.

"This is fabulous," she said, putting the chapter down.

"True." He smiled, pulling her plate to him and picking at her largely untouched dinner. "Lord, but you're insatiable, Louey." He twined a generous amount of her pasta around his fork.

"Yeah, I can never believe how rude my table manners are." She watched as Clay dangled a strand of her spaghetti in the air and leaned his head back, dropping it into his mouth. "You can't believe the number of times I've been asked to leave restaurants," she added dryly.

He wiped his mouth with the back of his hand, haughtily. "I wouldn't know." She snorted. "So you think it's the most brilliant thing you've ever read?"

"Tolerable," she said. "Now and then a line or two isn't too offensive." She pulled her dinner toward her and surveyed it with distaste. "Did I really eat this?"

"No, that was me. So you think it'll win all awards hands down and I won't have to sell my body anymore?"

"But that's your destiny, Clay." She affected a pained expression. "If you really cared about art, you wouldn't fight it."

"Was that a yes?"

"All right"—she gave in. "Satin sheets will be hung at half mast all over town." She toyed with the food on her plate. "I don't suppose you'd like to slam the rest of this down?"

"What do you *take* me for?"

"Trash." She looked on as he pulled the dish back and calmly finished her meal. "Everyone knows it, and it's time you did, too."

"I don't keep you around for your insights, missy—just your sweet nature."

She grabbed an olive. "Ditto, pruneface," she said, stuffing it into his mouth. "Now don't you think it's time you decided what I want for dessert?"

The thing that surprised Louey most about the months she'd worked with Clay was how easy it was to spend time with him. Often when she came to work and shuffled through her pile of messages, the only one that didn't make her shudder was from Clay.

"Tell me why I don't mind getting calls from him, no matter how busy I am," she asked one morning, bringing Kevin tea.

"Compulsive blabber?" he suggested.

She didn't even mind it when Clay talked her into holding their discussions over drinks or dinner. "It's not as if I don't like boys," she mused. "I like them." She stared down at a giant doughnut in his hand.

"You like the ones who blush like pretty girls," said Kevin, handing her some slightly sticky galleys to be sent for quotes. "We've all seen how you tease them."

"We can't agree on everything." She shook a finger at him. "Just because your own tastes border on . . ."

"Sublime?"

It puzzled her; she'd never found straight men that interesting for more than short periods of time, and sooner or later—usually sooner—they always came around to making a pass. (It had happened too often to surprise her. The number of males who were genuinely baffled when she took their hands from her hips or waist made her wonder what other women's responses to such tactics were, and if any man had ever been rejected before she'd come along.) With Clay, though, no rules seemed to apply. She had no precedent for their friendship.

"I've seen boys with just his kind of charm," said Kevin.

"Seen?" she snorted. "Nice euphemism." Why didn't Clay fit any pattern she had come across, straight or gay? "He's not one of those suave guys," she went on, "who keep doing you favors—until you find out why." She handed him the galleys with a pile of letters to be typed. "You, for instance."

Kevin laughed. "What I think," he said, "is that this polite-guy stuff is camouflage. He's a brute at heart—you wait and see."

"You like that kind, eh?" Louey turned to rewrite jacket copy for three books someone had mistakenly placed in their science-fiction line.

Several hours later Kevin returned to slip the heavily rewritten pages from beneath her elbow. "May I?" She nodded, covering her eyes. "I think we've done more than enough here, thank you." Her shoulders shook. "By the way, I've solved the Clay conundrum, if you're interested." Louey looked up at him, curious. "He's a simple, sweet, but spineless child who gets crushes on inaccessible women to avoid facing his own true sexuality."

"I don't think that's it," she said, "but let's just ask him, shall we?" She picked the phone up, and Kevin fled her office in mock terror.

It had been Louey's idea to transpose Clay's theories about love to fiction. "I sense a closet novelist lurking inside that shameless body," she'd said, and Clay had to admit she'd been right. Nothing could have prepared him for the way he lost himself in his creations, characters who wouldn't exist without him. And Louey called him "a born writer": fresh, funny, original, she said. The book (which she referred to as *Bright Lights, Hot Pussy*) still expressed his thesis about love, but she had helped him create a male character who embodied its follies and aspirations. "Why not make the narrator a boy with a lot of talent and a bright future," she suggested, "who keeps forestalling his own potential by becoming obsessed with one woman after another, mistaking the passion each provokes in him for the heightened life experience he's seeking?"

Why the hell hadn't he thought of it himself? "You could even salvage your research," she added, "give the hero signs he's on the right track—you know, ironic proof from movies, songs and books that love is more important than achievement." By offsetting his hero with characters who tried to restore him to a life of conventional accomplishment, Clay was able to voice his ambivalence far more subtly than his essay had allowed. And there was great fun in creating the women his hero longed for—laying out a portrait of Manhattan as he'd first seen it gave him a nearly malicious satisfaction. Louey had a few sly ideas of her own, as well—especially as to where his hero should meet women.

I met Mimi in a small dark room. I was riding up in the elevator of the tallest—and the first—office building I'd been in since arriving in New York. The one suit I owned was newly pressed and on my back, and although the building was (if anything) overly air-conditioned, my nerves were making me uncomfortably warm.

At the twenty-fifth floor, the elevator stopped, and all the other people filed out, leaving me to my thoughts. The door was closing when a husky voice called out, "Could you hold it?!" I stared at the air for a split second, then moved to hit the "open" button when a stocking-clad leg stuck its way into the door and prevented it (with no little pain to its owner, I imagined) from closing.

He didn't know what he had done to deserve the attention she'd shown him. Her willingness to take time out from what he knew was an insanely busy schedule to go over the most minute problem he might have with his material, the most inane question, seemed to transcend mere mortal patience. And the way her mind always came up with the answer to illuminate his difficulties was remarkable. He couldn't match the feeling he got when he showed her a batch of pages and her face lit up with pleasure, letting him know he was on the right track. Perversely he even enjoyed it when she criticized him, as if she'd understood better than he what he'd meant to say.

I pushed the button decisively, as if to make up for my delay. The door opened, and I faced a woman in an evening dress. A spectacular woman, actually, nearly six feet tall, all legs and flashing eyes and brazen shoulders and hips.

"Thanks." She grinned conspiratorially, then looked me up and down. *"Interview, eh?"*

I gave her the same treatment. "Convention, eh?" I said.

She laughed, raucously—hardly the kind of sound I would have expected from someone who had walked off the cover of Vogue. *"Nothing gets by you, does it, honey?" she said.*

Two things happened next: I sneezed and the elevator came to a thudding stop.

The only real problem was the ending. Louey was partial to the unexpected twist, but as yet neither of them had come up with anything inspired. Clay couldn't decide just how to bring his hero's plight to a resolution; simply having him continue his fruitless search for validation in physical bliss with women seemed inconclusive and unsatisfying, while providing him a pat resolution—like a woman who fulfilled all his dreams—seemed a cheap trick that betrayed his thesis. He considered having the character suddenly and unaccountably in the arms of one of his male friends—the biggest protester against the hero's quest for meaning, say—just to satisfy Louey's sense of the absurd, but he suspected this was a private joke few besides Louey would appreciate.

My companion looked on in amusement as I played with the buttons. We couldn't be stuck.

"You may as well give up," she said. "Once it sticks, it stays stuck until the repairmen come to fix it."

"But I have an interview in fifteen minutes. We can't just stay here!"

She shook her head. "Doesn't look promising."

I moved to ring the emergency button, but a surprisingly strong hand covered mine and pulled me away. "Calm down," she said. "Listen, there's nothing we can do but wait, so we may as well accept it and make the best of the situation."

"Great," I said. "How do you propose to make the best of three feet of space, no air, and nothing to do?"

"Depends on how you look at it." With this, she slid to the floor, slipping off her shoes with a sigh of relief. *"I've been dying to get out of these for hours. In fact, this whole ensemble is more than I can stand for one more minute."* Before I could blink, she was stripping off the charcoal stockings and then unzipping the tiny strapless dress. I could hardly believe my eyes.

"You can't be serious," I managed.

"Why's that?" A smile played over her lips as she rose and inched out of the tight dress, revealing a breathtaking collection of flesh and bones.

"Look," I said. *"I hope you don't mind, but I'd really rather—"*

"Aren't you feeling a bit . . . warm?" she asked. My throat was parched suddenly, and when I tried to answer, no sound came out. She scolded me with an outstretched finger, then moved it so that she was tracing the inside of my collar, toying with the buttons of my shirt.

"Are you crazy?" I pushed her hand away.

"Now, now," she murmured, *"you don't want to get overheated."* She slipped the jacket off my shoulders; I looked around the elevator for escape. Next thing I knew, she'd moved so close her breasts were pressing against me. My heart beat wildly as my nipples strained against the thin silk of my shirt as if to meet hers. Her hands came around me, barely skimming the surface of my body, unbuttoning my shirt. I stood frozen as she let my pants slide to the floor. I stared, wide-eyed, into what seemed to be a normal, sane face—my breath was coming in short gasps now. Her tongue slipped into my mouth, licking the soft inside of each lip, and then—

"I can't stand another minute of this." Kevin put down the mock chapter. Louey's face was red. "I'm going to die."

"But not alone," said Louey, her stomach sore from laughing. "Lucky everyone's gone home, or we'd be fired."

"Don't you think they know the reverence with which you treat your authors?" Kevin rose and got his things together. "You're not fooling anyone, dollface."

"That's what I hired *you* for, isn't it?" He put his coat on. "Walking home?" His face lit up. The two of them walked home together with a frequency that scandalized (and baffled) the whole office, but Kevin never failed to beam at her suggestion, as if the occasion might not come his way again. "Need protection?"

"I thought you'd never ask," said Kevin.

I broke away from her, moving to the farthest corner of the elevator and turning my back. Was she crazy? I peered over my shoulder; except for the fact of her complete nakedness, she might just as well have been a corporate executive waiting to interview me herself. I knelt, giving myself a serene mental picture to focus on, stretching my foot out to reclaim my pants.

Strange hands softly stole over my back, tracing the muscles to make me shiver. Soft breasts pressed against me and a hot tongue began lapping at my neck as if it was the most natural thing in the world for a stranger to do. As lethally skilled fingers crept down the front of me, I realized I was losing what little grip on rational thought I had managed to retain. After a few more moments of this, I realized I had no choice but to turn around and see what she could possibly have in mind for me.

"Creatures from Mars," Kevin called straight men. "So," he asked after they'd been walking for some time, "having dinner with the New Age Man?" She nodded. "Again? What do you see in him?" A painstakingly well-dressed executive passed, his lip curling at the sight of Kevin, who glanced at Louey, rolling his eyes. "That boy's far too nice and pretty to be truly straight," he added.

"Somehow I don't think he'd agree."

"I can see I'm going to need to have some words with him. He's ruining your reputation."

"All he wants from me are my brilliant insights."

"Poor child." Kevin covered his eyes. "How little you know of the world."

She laughed. In a moment they'd arrived at Kevin's building. "Need anything before I go?" he asked. "Illegal drugs, fresh weapons?"

She declined politely. "Now go make yourself irresistible."

"That should take some doing," he said. "But keep a kind thought."

It made no sense, thought Louey as she walked the rest of her way home: Clay simply shouldn't be someone she could spend effortless hours with. On all the basics they were as different as two people could be. No doubt he'd been raised to have contempt (or at best pity) for everything she stood for, everything she was. How could he know what it was like to be a woman, Jewish, gay? Christ, she thought, he wasn't even middle-class.

So why was she so comfortable with him? It baffled her. He seemed delighted by her in a purely selfless way—and he was so soft-spoken that often his wry humor caught her totally off-guard. He had none of the neurosis she'd always considered a necessary part of the urban personality she otherwise adored. Was it possible that someone could be intelligent and worldly without being frantic and intense or temperamental and unrelentingly self-involved? He's so much *fun*, she thought ruefully, shaking her head. She'd never known a person so apparently without conceit or ego, so agreeable without being spineless or dull.

It was true she'd never known anyone really rich before; perhaps wealth gave one the luxury of selflessness. She could only speculate, however, as Clay was reluctant to talk about money, his family, or anything truly personal. He was curious about her, she knew, and she spoke easily about her childhood, her theories, her foolish aspirations.

One topic was never broached, however: her love life, and her past with Mia. She knew he wanted more than anything to ask but wouldn't dare pry into her private life. She wondered if she'd ever want to tell him about Mia, if she'd ever be able to talk about it dispassionately, especially to someone like Clay. Still, she thought, as long as he hoarded his own secrets, he could hardly expect her to reveal hers.

Clay was awakened from a late night's work by the tail end of his father's voice on his machine. It was unusual for him to sleep through the phone's ringing, unheard of to sleep through a message. Yet lately it had become harder and harder to wrench himself from sleep. Despite the high of working on the book with Louey, he'd begun to find himself slipping into melancholy with increasing frequency. As he considered the third paternal wedding party in three years (this one no doubt with a pre-teen—his father's mates had been getting progressively nearer his own age), he realized why he'd been so morose the past few weeks. He dialed Louey's number.

"I've been calling all your other authors and telling them you're dead."

"Again?"

"I just thought you should know."

"Kevin?!" Louey called, and Kevin poked his head into her office. "Do we know a Pamela Kelly Boone III? She seems to feel she has some business with us."

"We don't associate with white trash," Kevin said. She handed him the receiver. "I'm terribly sorry, but Miss Mercer is no longer with Regent Books," he explained sweetly.

"I'm afraid we couldn't put up with her kleptomania any longer."

"Nancy Reagan, please," Clay said.

"Speaking."

"Let's talk about those dresses, babe. I mean, put a little meat on those bones! You look like a carcass."

"Ron likes me this way," Kevin said smugly.

"And who can blame him? God"—Clay sighed—"if only he did appreciate the likes of you, we'd be better off."

"Tell me, is there any reason I should give you back to Louey?"

"How does eight million dollars sound?"

"Reason enough." Kevin handed back the phone. A moment later he had vacated Louey's office and left Clay to see how she would respond to his latest plot development.

The past six months working with Louey had been more satisfying than he'd imagined possible, that was what was getting to him. That the project might be nearing its conclusion meant he'd no longer have any excuse to see her as he did now—so often that she seemed the most constant presence in his life. The thought depressed him beyond words. He'd never had a friend like her: so quick, so interested in wildly different things, as able to be transformed into a silly, giddy child as she was capable of sudden depths of understanding that made him feel almost in awe of her.

"I'm calling with a proposition," he said now.

"You mean the complete annihilation of my other authors was mere fabrication?" She sounded disappointed. "And I was so happy for a time . . ."

He hesitated: would she be offended by his invitation? "Actually, I wasn't calling about business, Louey. It seems my father is throwing a party for my stepmother—the third in a continuing series—and I was wondering if you'd consider being my escort."

She was silent so long that he wondered if he'd made one step too many over the line of their professional relationship. His spirits sank. She obviously had no interest in him as a friend, apart from their work together.

"When?" her voice came, interrupting his thoughts.

"Uh—next Monday, actually; it's at my father's tastelessly overfurnished apartment on Gramercy Park."

"How *is* your father?" she said.

He laughed. "Asks after you constantly."

"How formal would I have to be?"

"Oh, I'll get you a dress—"

She interrupted him, but he silenced her protests, for the first time almost eagerly anticipating what lay ahead. With Louey, being in his father's home might actually prove interesting. Whatever would she make of his family?

"You're crazy," she said, laughing, "and I have to get back to work. Go call Audrey Hepburn and buy *her* a dress. I'll talk to you later, Clay."

Smiling, he hung up. Brushing aside a possible explanation for his sudden high spirits as quickly as it arose, he ran his fingers through his hair and turned to brave the streets of New York.

The weekend was beautiful, clear and unusually warm for spring. Clay's cab maneuvered through the narrow streets bustling with people dressed in shirtsleeves, sitting on apartment stoops or walking around to soak up the sudden wealth of sunlight. As he looked out the car window, the pent-up energy that always burst forth from the city with the first sign of warm weather was threatening to reach a fever pitch.

Louey lived in a tiny walk-up apartment in a neighborhood Clay wouldn't have chosen to pass through voluntarily in daylight, much less picked to live in. He rang her buzzer, looking at his watch. It was two o'clock.

No answer: Clay cursed his impulsiveness. He should have called her first. If he'd come earlier, or called, he might have caught her in. Halfheartedly he pressed the button again, glancing down the street. He had just turned to leave when the return buzzer came, letting him in.

Clay scaled the five flights of stairs, not fully certain it was Louey who had responded to his buzz. Sometimes in apartments like these anyone who heard a buzzer would answer it; he'd been greeted on other stairs by unfamiliar grizzled faces, bathrobes, curlers.

He rang her doorbell. There was the sound of movement inside, and a faint "Who is it?" The voice was barely awake, incredulous that someone might be there.

"It's Clay, Louey, Clayton Lee. Have I come at a bad time?"

She opened the door, wearing a dark blue robe several sizes too big that she'd clearly flung on hastily. (It slipped off one shoulder to bare the pale, creamy skin of a nine-year-old.)

"I woke you."

"No, that's okay," she said vaguely, yawning. "I should be up, anyway." She blushed. "Come on in." He followed her through the narrow hallway into a small room dominated by a disheveled bed.

"Do you always sleep this late?" he asked. Two o'clock beat even his own record.

"What are you doing here?" She was starting to wake up and peered at him suspiciously. "Don't you normally call before you visit someone?"

"I should have given you some warning. I'm sorry." Curled up on a corner of the bed, pressed against the wall with her legs crossed yoga-style under her, she looked like a Botticelli angel on the verge of dropping off again. The robe had slipped so that her legs were bared up to the thigh. He was suddenly struck with a fierce longing to disrobe her completely and ease the fatigue off her face. Jesus! He must be out of his mind. He averted his eyes, concentrating on her face. Her eyes flashed sarcasm and annoyance.

"You're really having a good time with this, aren't you?" she said. She was now fully awake. "This is the limit, this beats even my 3 a.m. calls from Bambi."

It had never occurred to him that she would get so upset. Her eyes were blazing. He hardly knew what to say to her. "I'm sorry," he tried finally. (Her jaw remained set.) "You're absolutely right. I've been relying on you as if you have nothing else to do but help me. I'll try to be more considerate from now on."

She waited for him to say more, but he'd finished, and they sat in silence. She laid her hands flat on her knees, studying them intently. It occurred to him that her outburst had taken her as much by surprise as it had him. "Well!" She took a breath. "Now that was fun."

"I take it you're not much for mornings," he said, relieved. "Species *Homo nocturnus*, eh?"

"Watch who you're calling homo, pal." She made a face at him.

"So what do you want to do today?" Clay said. "I was thinking we might get you that dress."

"Pinhead," she said, stretching. "For a start, I'd like to take a shower." She slumped farther into the mattress, sighing loudly as if the thought of moving was too painful to bear. "I do have time for a shower, don't I?" She seemed completely oblivious to him physically, as if he presented not the slightest threat—or interest—to her. It was an odd sensation. Here Clay was, acutely conscious of her body, small, compact, disarming, and very nearly revealed to him. It unnerved him; no doubt she could have dropped her robe and stood naked in front of him without giving a thought to his presence. "Clay?"

"Don't be silly," he said. "Of course you have time for a shower. Go ahead with whatever you were planning to do before I came."

"Now there's a novel idea." She gave him a dirty look, going into the bathroom. A minute later Clay heard the water being turned on, and then the sound of a body entering it. No point in imagining her robe dropping to the floor and the water hitting her bare flesh, the small rounded breasts, the little belly, the smooth, full thighs and dampening triangle between them. He wasn't a masochist—or a fool. There was nothing here for him. It was true he'd never met anyone quite like her—his life had been excruciatingly predictable until he'd come to know her—but he knew better than to expect more from her than occasional distraction from whatever dismal future Fate had planned for him.

He was completely unprepared for the sight of her emerging from the bathroom. Wrapped in a white towel, she shook her hair dry, bending her head slightly to one side and then another as the fine hair stood out in spikes. He wasn't ready for the pang he felt when she twisted to towel the back of a knee and revealed a glimpse of pink breast. What was the meaning of the involuntary quickening of his heart as she walked past him and he inhaled shampoo and clean skin? He wasn't here for that. The smile froze on his face as he tried to implant some reason on his mind, to forestall his senses. She hadn't the slightest interest in him; she would never have the slightest interest in him, not that way. He could not fathom how his practical nature had so abruptly and thoroughly sabotaged him. Surely he could shake this folly; he was merely reacting to externals, to the physical body before him.

"What are you smiling like that for?" she said, somehow slipping into some pants without revealing any more of herself. "You have to be the gooniest boy I've ever met." She went to her closet, dropping the robe and pulling a jersey over her head. The skin of her back was pale and smooth; she was probably smooth all over. The sight of her shoulder blades straining together as she put her arms into the sleeves tugged at him. He had an urge to place one cool hand in the center of her back, between the warm wings. (He could see where this was leading him.)

"Have you known many?" His voice was constricted; he cleared his throat.

She was silent. "Some," she said. She looked out the window briefly. "Not the way you mean, I suppose."

"Lots of women?"

"No," she said. "Not lots."

"More than one?" She didn't answer. "What was it like?" he blurted in a hoarse whisper. "How did you meet her?"

Her face took on the same expression he'd seen at the restaurant those years ago: a kind of amused misery, as if she were mocking herself for the extent of the pain she felt. "Who?" she said, choking on her next word, "Mia?" A look of horror crossed her features as her eyes suddenly filled. She turned abruptly and went back into the bathroom.

Clay sat breathing as heavily as if he'd just raced to slip through the doors of a departing subway, missing the train by mere seconds. The afternoon lay around him in a shambles. How was he going to get through casually buying her a dress now? The prospect was so far beyond his imagining that he could only wait, his mind blank, until she came out of the bathroom to face him.

He lay, spread-eagled on a cool white table, arms extended high above his head, crossed at the wrists. The sensation coming from his nipples was agonizing yet almost unendurably pleasurable. When he tried to reach down to stop it, his hands wouldn't oblige. They were tied, somehow, bound with a soft, unyielding fabric. He lifted his head. She was tonguing his nipples, one, the other, slowly, excruciatingly slowly, like a cat lapping up milk. Only she wasn't a cat and her tongue felt like liquid fire, every so often yielding to a nip from her teeth. His whole body throbbed; his cock felt so inflamed he half expected to see it rise to monstrous proportions, like a creature from a horror movie. Every flick of her tongue had his body twitching. Wouldn't she touch him?

Without warning, she slowed her pace. Rather than give him relief, the now-rare flicks drove him near frenzy, causing every nerve in his body to shriek. How could she be doing this with just her tongue, with just his nipples? Wouldn't she ever release him from this torture? Stop? Let him go?

One hand idly brushed his thigh as if by accident. He groaned, twisting his head. If only he could loosen his hands, touch her. He tried to slide his knee up her smooth curves but he discovered his legs were also bound. He was her prisoner. She could taunt him for hours and he'd never be able to lift a finger to stop her.

One hand slid up, grazing his bare chest and stomach; the other moved down, a trail of heat and damp. A brief caress of his inflamed core left him gasping, straining toward her for more. Abruptly she stopped, leaving his body throbbing. Then, after an agonizing moment, she began the most tentative exploration of the surface of his skin. Just when he thought he could take no more, she lowered herself onto him, engulfing him in satiny heat, plunging his tortured body over the edge.

Clay woke, crying out as passion racked his body in an arc. The breaths came from him in painful gasps. When the beating of his heart finally slowed, he opened his eyes to peer at the lighted dial: 4:30. He fell back onto his mattress, wondering if he'd ever sleep a peaceful night again.

"I feel like a drag queen," she said, getting into the cab and sliding next to him.

Several drinks had enabled Clay to pick Louey up without too much difficulty, although the grim set of her jaw sent his hopes for the evening plummeting. She looked beautiful in the dress they had picked out, a rich blue that brought out the color of her troubled eyes and the rosy glow of her pale skin. The narrow waist emphasized the curves she normally camouflaged, her lovely breasts confronting him defiantly, like an assault. Closing the car door, he wiped a small patch of moisture from his brow.

"You look wonderful," he said. Was he imagining the slur of his words? He couldn't be that drunk.

"Right. I can see how I did so nicely not owning a formal dress all these years. Got any drugs?"

He stared at her, instinctively patting his pockets. "Uh, well, no, I—"

"Kidding!" She laughed at his expression, and he relaxed, trying to laugh with her. If only he could get his muscles to work normally. All he had to do was control himself, put this foolishness out of his mind. (Easy as ripping the lungs from his body.)

He had spent the last week unable to get the picture of Louey out of his head, running over and over the vision of her half naked as she'd opened her door to him; the unfamiliar flash of rage in her eyes when he'd awakened her, the image of her eyes filling as she fled the room.

That night he'd blundered home after their agonizing shopping spree. Once she'd emerged from the bathroom, red-eyed and thin-lipped, they'd barely spoken four sentences to each other, avoiding serious topics like two people after a collision who might shatter at the slightest hint of pressure. She'd tried on dress after dress; in between fittings, Clay had had to close his eyes, willing himself far away, anywhere but here with this girl who left him so precariously balanced in reality, so aching and bewildered. No woman had ever made him feel so lost—his brief obsession with the beautiful Mia paled to invisibility in comparison with the unheralded passion he'd developed for the woman she'd jilted. This tiny girl he'd come to rely on completely—what had he done to reward her for her attentions? He had not even been able to keep his lust under control, lust for a woman for whom the thought of male bodies was at best irrelevant. He'd doused himself in alcohol in an orgy of self-recrimination and gone out cold, only to find her image floating before him night after night. Her body had taunted him in so many infinite variations he wondered if he'd become truly depraved.

Now, riding in a car with her, he felt removed, a detached observer. He responded to her wit intellectually, taking note of his amusement as if it belonged to someone else.

"You look tired," she said softly. Her tone caused something to tear inside him; with some effort he kept his breathing even. They'd only known each other in the context of a business project, he told himself; it was the artificial intimacy of a long train ride or joint kidnapping that had provoked such feelings of kinship. This physical business would pass, and then perhaps they could truly become friends.

By the time they arrived at the party, he had convinced himself there was still some chance that the evening could turn out a success. This notion was quickly dispelled upon seeing his father, who took one look at Louey and seemed to draw upon his full capacity for disdain. Clay was stunned. What possible fault could his father find with Louey, to be regarding her like that? She looked lovely, obviously spirited, intelligent. Was it that Clayton still harbored some notion of pairing him with a woman of the "proper" background and ambition, someone who would ease him into working for the family firm? He introduced them, but this only made matters worse; upon hearing Louey described as his son's editor, Clayton hardened his face to granite. Louey was polite, if a bit puzzled by his coldness, but before Clay could think to steer Louey away from his father, the older man had excused himself and retreated without warning.

"Well!" Louey said, turning to him. "I think he liked me!" She grinned wryly, but Clay hadn't recovered quickly enough to answer. "Must be the horns . . ."

Then the worst possible thing that he would ever have imagined happened. The young capitalist who had been enterprising enough to bring Mia to the last neo-maternal party nearly three years earlier showed up, with Mia on his arm once again. Clay felt the room begin to spin as he took in the sight of Mia arriving in a ravishing glow and obscene gown. He turned to Louey, who paled, faltering. He took her arm to keep her from falling, grasping it like a life preserver, but it was clearly too late for salvation of any kind.

"Excuse me—" Louey blurted, and flung herself from the room, taking refuge in the kitchen adjoining the main hall. He followed her blindly, uttering an apology, but the face she turned to him was ghostly, pitiful, halting his speech. "Please, Clay, I just—can you leave me alone for a minute? I promise I'll be back as soon as—please?" He obeyed, following stray relatives from table to table. He drank from first one bar and then the next, but it didn't seem to have any effect on him; he was as sober as he'd ever been. People he knew came up to him while he waited for Louey to emerge, but he was unable to muster the energy to make even small talk. His father's lips grew thinner by the minute, but every time he started to approach Clay, his lovely bride steered him toward another pillar of society. How was he going to make it up to Louey? She would think he'd done it on purpose.

Mia was now speaking to one of the men carrying hors d'oeuvres, Clay noted, making his way toward her. Before he'd reached her, she had gone outside to where her date stood smoking on the terrace. Clay followed, stopping just inside the door and listening like a child molester.

"What's the matter, Mia?" her companion asked. "You've been so down lately."

"I've always thought it rude to be too happy in front of other people," Mia said, taking his cigarette. "Oh, but this will interest you." She exhaled smoke. "I saw the hugest cock in America last night."

"Pardon?"

"My next-door neighbor's shower broke; so I offered him mine. Before I knew it—well, I've never seen anything like it. I tried to explain that I was a vegetarian, but he didn't seem to understand. I don't know how I managed to get out alive."

"What's his number?" the man asked. Mia laughed, and her friend put out the cigarette. "Really, Mia, you just can't leave cocks lying around like that without even giving them a chance to show what they can do."

"Honey, I don't even want to know their names, much less find out what they do."

At this Clay bolted back inside the apartment, his head pounding. He had to save Louey from this person. The throbbing in his brain refused to subside even as Louey emerged from the kitchen. He headed toward her, as his father appeared like a bad vision, cutting him off. From the corner of his eye he could see Mia coming in from the terrace, approaching Louey.

Escape seemed impossible. Louey started to move unsuspectingly toward Mia, but Clay caught her arm; he had to save her. "Father," he began, "I don't think you were treating Louey with the courtesy she deserves." His father raised an eyebrow in surprise and disdain. Clay could feel Louey's puzzled eyes on him, but suddenly he wanted nothing more than to wipe the smug look off his father's face. "You'd better show her more respect," he said, "because I plan to marry her." He smiled, like the good son he was.

Clay had a long meeting with his hangover, but by noon they were able to find Louey's home phone number. She answered on the second ring.

"Why do I get the feeling you don't appreciate my sense of humor?" he started.

"You and I have different definitions of fun," Louey answered.

This was going to be considerably more difficult than he'd anticipated, judging by her tone. "Say, Louey," he should ask, "are there a lot of Communists in your family?" ("Hordes," she'd answer.) Then he could point out that, as her family surely also included many Jews and maybe even some poor people, the notion of marriage to him was a heaven-sent opportunity to torment his father, to repay his snubbing her. Yet all signs indicated that she'd failed to see the irony in the situation. "At least let me explain," he said. "I'm so sorry—I had no idea that Mia would be there."

"I'd rather not talk about Mia. Anyway, I'm sure you think this is all terribly—"

"You can't tell me you don't see the humor in it. I mean, objectively speaking, it would be a perfect setup. You'd get to torture the rich . . ."

"And give myself a thrill as well? Since every woman dreams of marriage?"

"No, that's not—"

"Clay, you're alarming me. I've really got to hang up now. Don't think it hasn't been a dream."

This was not going as he'd planned; if only she would let him explain about Mia. "I'm sorry I got you in the middle of this, and I'm sorry you're upset." She was silent. "Look, you don't know what it's like to be the golden hope of the family firm."

"What about all those little pinko Jew babies he'd be expecting us to give him?"

"Don't you see, he'd be relieved we didn't!" He covered his eyes; he was babbling. "Louey, I was pissed at the way he was acting. I wanted to hurt him, not you." He swallowed. "This is why I stay away from my family."

"Well," she said. "I hope you find someone to make you happy."

"I'm not looking for—" To his astonishment, the phone had gone dead in his hand. She had hung up on him.

He placed the receiver in its cradle. This was taking things a bit too far, he thought. It was understandable that she was upset about Mia, though, strictly speaking, it wasn't his fault. Yet to hang up on him because of a silly joke anyone with a shred of humor could appreciate—it wasn't like her at all. It was crazy.

Still, as he considered the chill in her voice, he wondered if he had just destroyed any chance he might have of seeing her again. As he considered what this turn of events signified, and what she now seemed to feel for him, he was filled with growing horror at the realization that he had somehow fallen completely, hopelessly in love with her.

I met Lulu in a small, dark room. I had just managed to survive an unsuccessful flight to Paris with a small percentage of the aircraft's passengers, and though I seemed to have passed out from the sheer thrill of the crash, when I woke up I was neatly tucked into a small bed, somehow completely on my own. I sat up, then fell back in a swoon. The door opened.

"Still among the living?" said a tall dark stranger, peering down at me with a lack of respect for the injured I hastened to chastise her for. Yet when I saw her face, I found myself unable to speak; surely this was no doctor, this was a goddess impersonating a doctor, a hallucination. She was so beautiful I felt dazed just looking at her, and when her face lit up in a smile, I could feel my temperature rising. There was obviously something wrong with my bodily functions.

"Let me have a look at you," she murmured, an unprofessional gleam in her eye. Tugging at the covers, she unveiled my apparently unmarred body, which had been clothed in some sort of tasteful equivalent of a burlap sack. Taking a pair of scissors from her pocket, she neatly cut the gown down the middle, startling me. Then she pulled the sides apart, exposing me completely.

"Uh—" I started, but she silenced me with a stern shake of her head, continuing to study my naked body intently as if searching for subtle signs of internal injury. "Am I—"

Sometimes Louey would be walking down a street and catch a glimpse of someone she was sure was Mia—it didn't even have to be a physical resemblance, but just the way a thin dress shimmered, clinging to a body as if there were nothing underneath, as if the dress had only come to life when slid on over Mia's flesh. She had a way of making clothes seem slightly sordid. Even in a plain black sheath she gave off the impression she'd just finished having sex, for hours—standing up.

She gingerly began to press my flesh, making small sounds as if she were making a discovery with each touch. Her hands were surprisingly warm and gentle, and I closed my eyes. Her palms swept over me, pressing, smoothing. This wasn't accomplishing what she had in mind, I thought.

Next she was brushing her fingernails across my chest. My eyes flew open. "Does that hurt?" she said softly. I started to protest, but she covered my mouth with one hand. I began to feel dizzy as one hand warmed my lips and the other continued to make its way down my body. "How about that?" she said. "That feel painful? Sore?"

I didn't seem to be able to answer coherently, and before I realized what she was doing, she had moved her hands down my legs, squeezing softly. "Am I hurting you?" she asked, pressing the flesh of my calves and the insides of my thighs with an attention that went beyond professionalism. "Feel okay? There? How about there?"

"Uh, okay." She reached between my legs, ignoring my widened eyes. "I don't think it's necessary to—"

"I'm the doctor," she said harshly. "Do you want to let a serious injury go untreated?" I gave up, closing my eyes again

LOONGLOW

as her fingers began to play my flesh with fatal accuracy. "That hurt?" she murmured, pressing. "That? That hurt? Does that?"

Her hands continued for what seemed like hours. "Oh, God," I told her. She smiled at me. "God, that hurts."

With the advent of Sales Conference, Louey realized that life as she knew it was soon going to be worse than ever. Twice a year the company geared up to put the best possible face on the season's books to the salesmen who went out and sold them around the country, and twice a year office insanity escalated beyond all normal bounds. Why was it, Louey wondered, that she never remembered how bad it got until the madness came around again? This year the management was even more hysterical than ever, as if there were some serious question about the company's future. Louey (and most of the staff) had been privy to what seemed like daily human sacrifices. No one knew why their lovely boss needed fresh new victims every morning; most of them just held their breath and prayed not to be chosen. Though Daisy prided herself on being "one of the few truly Christian publishers around," she seemed to thrive on playing the lion. So far Louey hadn't been called to The Office, but that was sheer blind luck, she knew.

She had fifteen books this season. It had been bad enough when she'd had half as many. She had to start rejecting authors, she realized; her work life had gotten completely out of hand. Why did she always forget how authors could transform themselves from competent professionals to small, dependent children in a matter of days? The sheer volume of work was eroding her usual goodwill; the closer Sales Conference approached, the more frayed her nerves became. Fran Lebowitz was right: childhood was the last time you could be truly happy to hear that the phone was for you.

Kevin became increasingly protective toward her, but the work was taking its toll on him as well. Occasionally he would even make mistakes, which was completely out of character, and though they were usually minor, he flayed himself as if he couldn't comprehend how the person responsible for them had taken over his body.

"Get me out of here!" he wailed.

"Toto," she said, "where's Kansas?"

There were times Louey wondered if she could bear to continue at this job. Regent Books was considered one of the worst publishers in the business, it was true, but when you came right down to it, she wondered how many truly good ones there were. Nearly every publisher she'd met displayed some form of psychosis. (One man she knew threw bagels at his staff whenever sales of their biographies of criminals and courtesans were too low for his liking; another liked to corner unsuspecting females for coital bliss atop the carpet of the conference room where weekly editorial meetings were held.) Louey marveled that so many people incapable of civil conversation had managed to rise to positions of substantial power. Those publishers who were genuinely nice rarely had openings for new editors; once someone landed at a house at which it was actually pleasant to work, he rarely left. Louey wondered if she had the patience to wait through years of fighting off sexual assault or flying baked goods until she found a haven—if one actually existed.

When she seriously thought about quitting, however, she

had to admit that it would be even worse to have so much free time she'd be able to dwell on the subject of Mia round the clock. That she might be able to withstand the temptation to dwell on Mia every free second she got was utterly implausible; she'd proven that all too well.

Clay hadn't meant to hurt her, she knew, but she couldn't stop replaying the memory of that dumb-animal expression on his face, and then discovering the cause of it, Mia. How stupid could he be, not to consider the possibility that Mia might show up, since his father obviously knew her? The way he turned such a shamefaced red made it seem as if he had expected Mia to be there. Maybe she should have asked to hear the story he'd alluded to only once. (She always tried to resist any impulse to ask about Mia, to learn anything about her life when it touched someone else, since it could never again touch her.) Yet what use was there in trying to be rational? No matter what she did, Mia returned to haunt her. Mia was an addiction, clearly, like food or air. The thought that she would have to live without her, day in, day out, for the rest of her life, still had the power to incapacitate her.

"Why not try looking for someone new?" Kevin mentioned one afternoon.

"What, a stranger?" She stared as if he'd suggested homicide. "I wouldn't know what to do with my hands."

"I'm sure some nice girl would be happy to help you with that little problem." He smiled, opening a can of soda as he ogled the pedestrians strolling up Sixth Avenue. "Louey, it's not healthy to lock yourself up like this—your brains get fried. It's time to meet another sordid, flashy woman."

"And then come tell you everything?" she sneered.

"Just try to keep in mind I brought you up to be a lady." He ducked a flying paper bag.

.   .   .

The day came for the in-house run-through of book presentations for the spring list. Louey always dreaded these meetings; it was the closest thing to being called before the principal that adult life had to offer. She did fairly well once she got going; there was always some enjoyment in entertaining the staff, an audience eager to be amused. When Louey got to the podium to present her first book, she studied the silent faces, sensing welcoming anticipation.

In the middle of her presentation of a book about the rag trade (which Louey called *Garmentos from Hell*), an unexpected interruption came from Daisy, whose rages had thus far been restricted to the confines of her office. Without warning, she began to tear apart Louey's speech, the book (which Burt, the editor in chief, had bought and then dumped on her), even the author's physical dimensions. As she railed, Louey grew numb, trying to answer calmly. Unhappily, her replies only seemed to fuel the other woman's irritation. Finally Louey held her tongue, until the last outburst had run its course. Then she turned and made her way back to her seat.

The next few presentations went by in somewhat of a blur. It seemed to Louey that Daisy's further outbursts were just fainthearted versions of her attack on Louey. She did not think she was being overly sensitive in drawing this conclusion; no one in the room would meet her eye.

Returning to the podium was even worse. As she presented a riveting if bizarre biography of an unorthodox surgeon whose daughter Louey called "poodle girl—World's Tallest Mammal"—Daisy continued her vendetta. Louey didn't know why this behavior should surprise her; she'd seen enough convincing evidence of Daisy's penchant for abuse. (If anything it should be easier to endure than watch.) Yet somehow it grew harder each time to rise and go up to the front of the room. As she discussed a mercilessly satirical novel called *Great Big Hairdo*, Daisy retreated slightly, making a small joke at her expense without attacking the book itself. She could sense the room's poised anticipation and surprise at Daisy's sudden capitulation. Then the meeting was called for lunch.

Louey walked to her office in a daze, scarcely believing what had happened. Daisy's relish at humiliating others usually expressed itself publicly in random swipes, rarely a concentrated attack. It must have been her inability to feign immediate concession to Daisy's initial protests that had swelled the publisher's rage. Nor could Louey fathom that there had been no protest from any corner of the room. As she got her things together to go out, the editor in chief corralled her, asking her to lunch. She canceled the plans she'd made: perhaps Burt had some explanation for the day's events. She might even be fired. The thought made her slightly giddy.

As they walked to the restaurant, Burt remained silent, breaking his internal dialogue only to make the most trivial of small talk. He can't bear to tell me until we're in the restaurant, Louey thought. When they sat down, he ordered a drink, still silent; he couldn't bear to tell her without a drink, evidently.

At last it came. "I know you must be upset about this morning." She held her breath. "But in a way you asked for it." He took a sip of his drink.

"How?"

He studied his menu, clearing his throat. "There was something almost casual in your presentations. You weren't really selling your books." Her eyes widened. "I know you must be feeling bad," he hastened to assure her, yet he went on picking apart her performance, as if trying to convince himself of the inherent logic in the publisher's ravings.

"Oh?" The quiet sarcasm in her voice brought color to his cheeks. Was there any point in mentioning that books he'd bought had been among the ones Daisy had attacked? she wondered. He'd been silent in their defense as well as hers. She sighed: it was no use. Her boss was a man who prided himself on being keenly sensitive, more intrinsically humane than anyone alive. His taking her to lunch was some kind of symbolic sympathetic gesture, she could see, even as his words belied his actions. That he was fond of Louey didn't stop him from trying to make sense of this abuse of her; if it had truly been senseless, he could not have let it go and still consider himself a caring person.

After lunch (for which Louey could not bring herself to thank him), the meeting resumed. So, unfortunately, did the attack on Louey's presentations. How long had she worked at this place? she wondered. How was it this had never happened before?

By the time she reached a discussion of her twelfth book, the now all-too-familiar voice interrupted to explain that what might be of interest to "literary Jew faggots writing for *The Village Voice* wasn't of the slightest concern to normal people, who bought most books anyway."

At this, something in Louey broke. "I'm sorry you feel that way," she said. Burt stole a glance at his boss, reserving his opinion until Daisy made her next move. Louey drew her things together, sighing. "I can't speak for all the Jew faggots in the world, of course, but I doubt the people in this room have had much fun listening to you tear apart projects people have worked hard on. If you've got some problem with me, I don't think it's fair that all these people have to suffer for it."

A silence fell over the room. At last Daisy spoke. "Let's go on, shall we?" Her voice was polite. "I believe you're finished?"

Louey nodded, starting to make her way back to her seat.

Daisy stopped her. "I don't think we'll be needing you any further, Louey."

Pardon? Louey blinked. Uh, okay. With the hushed silence of an ambush ringing in her ears, she turned and walked out of the room and then the building.

Louey was walking back into her dorm room after her final freshman exam when her roommate took a rare break from her continuous phone calls to announce, "Your stepsister's here."

"Pardon me?" Louey said, but her roommate, already reabsorbed in conversation, didn't answer. Dumping her books in the outer closet, Louey opened the door to the bedroom adjoining her roommate's.

She should have had an inkling. Mia lay on her bed, idly reading an old draft of a paper she'd just finished. Louey went in and sat down on the floor, leaning against the wall across from Mia.

"Happy to see me?" Mia stretched, laying down the papers.

"What are you doing here?"

"Did I come at a bad time?" She grinned at Louey.

How had she managed so long without this sight? Louey wondered. It had been nearly a year since she'd touched (or even seen) Mia. "What are you doing here?" Her head was spinning.

"How'd you do on your finals?" Mia stroked her lower lip lazily, her eyes not leaving Louey's.

"Pretty well, I think." Her voice was shaky, and she cleared her throat. "Did you drive all the way out here?"

"You must have me confused with some other common trollop." Mia put a hand over her eyes and nestled against the pillows. "I hitched. One guy even took me two hundred miles out of his way. Wasn't that sweet?"

"From now on, he'll have his eyes glued to the side of the road looking for you."

"Tough break," said Mia softly, unbuttoning her shirt. Louey's heart stung in her chest. It didn't make sense, Mia here in her dorm room, lying on her bed, undressing. She'd wondered more than once if she'd imagined what had happened that bewildering afternoon. Mia bent to take her shoes off. "Is there something keeping you from leaping onto this bed, by the way?"

Louey went over to the bed and Mia pulled her down against her. It had been ten months since she'd kissed— since she'd seen Mia at all; with each kiss she banished weeks. Mia slipped her hands under her sweater, studying Louey's face as if looking for some transformation brought on by the separation or its cause. "You miss me?" she said, doing several things beneath the thin material that made it difficult to answer. Louey was breathing heavily; the blood seemed to be pumping in slow motion as she closed her eyes and yielded to Mia's hands. What was Mia doing here? It must have happened, then; she hadn't dreamed it. She couldn't believe that Mia had come here—for *her*?

"Loved your letters," she said, breaking away and getting off the bed. Mia gave her a child's truant grin as Louey went to her closet to change her clothes. (The only piece of mail Louey had received had been a gaudy postcard with Mia's uncontrolled scrawl explaining that the baby was fine but that Louey should send money for braces or risk having her child a marked woman for life.) Louey had tried to call, but Mia never seemed to be at school. Even at midterm she had had to learn from Mia's distantly contemptuous mother that her daughter had gone traveling with several friends.

"I notice you took advantage of your own ample opportunity to write," Mia said.

"I wrote you four letters, if you'll pardon my mentioning it. For all I know, you burned them."

"Sold 'em." Mia came up behind Louey, toying with her neck and sliding an arm around her waist. Louey shivered. "Made a tidy sum, by the way. You should just see the frilly little thing I bought with the money."

"Fetched a good price, did they?" But Mia didn't seem to want to talk, biting Louey's bare skin gently, cupping her shoulders. Louey cleared her throat.

"Porn's in great demand," Mia went on.

"You must have gotten the letter I meant for Mom."

At this Mia put both arms around her waist. Louey leaned back, unable to concentrate on anything but the sensation of Mia against her. She started to say something, but Mia's hands were moving across the front of her, making it difficult to think. "Uh, come here often?" she managed.

"Try to." Mia nibbled a trail down her back. "Wouldn't want you to get bored with all those coeds."

"You're so thoughtful," Louey said. "In fact, I've always felt—" But before she could finish, Mia was turning her around and soon it was all Louey could do to remain standing.

The next day Mia loaded Louey into the car she'd borrowed from Louey's brother. (The young man had been a complete fiction, as Louey should have suspected.) Once they hit the highway, Mia mentioned that she had discussed summer plans with Louey's family, who had casually let slip that they had never really liked Louey much anyway.

"That's a relief," Louey said.

"Which leaves the coast clear," Mia mentioned, weaving in and out between cars in breakneck fashion.

As they drove across the country, Mia became effervescent, almost childlike, filled with energy. She seemed barely able to contain herself, tugging Louey from one spot to the next, showing off her favorite sights as if they didn't exist until Louey saw them. Was being alone with someone always like this? Louey wondered. Did other people share this special, private heaven?

It was as if the blue of the sky, the friendliness of strangers, the mysteries of passion had been invented just for them. She couldn't believe how elated she was all the time, as if she'd never feel any emotion besides joy. She couldn't believe Mia could make her feel this way—that Mia could feel this way because of her.

If only the summer didn't have to end.

The day after the Fall, Louey came into work and started clearing out her office, piling books and papers, calendars and folders into boxes she had brought from home. As people started drifting into the office—first assistants, then their bosses—they soon formed a crowd around her door, watching her pack. She smiled ruefully at each of them, unaccustomed to her sudden notoriety. Around her, conversation was hushed, as if no one could fathom how things had abruptly come to such an end.

"Hello," the mournful voice of her now-former boss issued behind the mob. The crowd dispersed and she was left alone with him.

"Hi, Burt," she answered cheerfully, clearing the plants off her windowsill. Her boss sat down in the chair across from her, his silence heavy, fraught with accusation.

Louey gave in to the pressure of his gaze upon her back at last, sitting down.

"Well," he said, rubbing his hands down gray-clad legs. "You gave us quite a surprise yesterday."

"You and me both," she started, then reconsidered her next words. "I assume you'll want me to help break in my replacement—and I'll try to ease the transitional period for my authors over the next two weeks."

He averted his eyes. "That won't be necessary."

"What?" She frowned. He studied a corner of her office, silent. "I have to tell my authors and their agents what to expect. It's hard enough to leave them dangling, with sales conference just around the corner." (You should have thought of that, she could hear him thinking.) "I'm sorry I don't have more time to wrap things up."

He seemed intent on memorizing a spot slightly to the left of her shoulder. "They want you out by five."

Her jaw dropped. "Today?" He nodded, still not looking at her. "But that leaves everyone just—" She stopped. His tone was too flat; it was useless. How did he manage to be so cool so abruptly—when just the other day he'd laughed with her about an author and even grudgingly expressed approval of her work? "Are you sure you can find someone to help rip my books to shreds on such short notice?" He looked at her with mournful eyes. "Burt"—she bit her lip. "You can't pull the rug out from under so many people. Even if I could reach most of them today—" He was barely listening. "But they're the ones who are going to suffer," she trailed on, helpless.

"You knew it was a tough business when you took this job."

So she wasn't tough enough for it, she thought, was that the problem? "Did you ask Daisy for more time to make things easier for my authors?" He picked at the fabric of his suit jacket. "Have you been dissatisfied with my work?"

He rose. "Taking an attitude like that is counterproductive, Louey. There's no point in dwelling on side issues."

Before she could reply, he'd turned and left her office. Louey looked down at a half-packed box, her head filled with cotton. After a moment, she shook herself, reaching for the phone.

Once Louey had been walking, late at night, home from a party, when she'd found herself in sudden danger. Both she and Mia were just slightly drunk; when Mia stopped to buy some flowers, Louey went to buy some milk the next block up. She saw a young girl come out of the market just as she did, casually slipping something into her bag. An old woman standing nearby shouted, "Put that back!" and the girl broke into a run, putting the stolen package on the ground under a car. The store's two owners started after her, but without thinking Louey picked the package up and put it back. "She put it back," she said, and then the two men stopped, and the girl went free. Mia caught up with her and they began to walk, when Louey heard a noise. She turned and saw the girl, who had been joined by several boys.

"Why don't you mind your business?" the girl yelled, and Louey realized the girl was much more shabbily dressed than she'd first thought.

"What do you mean?"

"Did you ever think that might have been my dinner?"

"I put it back," she said, "so they wouldn't chase you." Mia glanced at her, surprised.

"All those guys would have found was what I bought," the girl said. "They'd look in the bag and wouldn't find it."

"Oh." She hadn't realized that the girl had never meant to give the package back; she'd been planning this, to put it down if she'd been caught, then come and get it later. "Sorry," she said, shrugging. Mia took her arm.

The two of them had walked half a block when someone started throwing cans at them. Louey turned: it was the girl, enraged, as if she blamed Louey for what had happened. Instinctively Louey started walking faster, but the cans still came, landing around their feet.

Without thinking, Louey turned. "Are you going to throw cans at us all the way up Broadway?"

The girl was at her side instantly, a bottle in her hand. Louey's eyes grew wide. "Don't you talk to me that way!" the girl shouted. "Are you crazy?" She waved the bottle right in Louey's face, then tapped the back of Louey's head with it as if just barely holding back from smashing it against her skull.

"Hey!" Mia said, grabbing the girl's arm violently. The muscles strained in both their arms; Louey could barely breathe. She couldn't believe she'd been so stupid, couldn't imagine how the night had come to this. The girl glared at Mia, her arm still poised, then turned to Louey.

"Don't you ever do a thing like that again," she spat out. Louey saw the bottle, thinking, All she had to do was shatter it against me, one two three. She felt her mind go numb. The girl said, "Meet you at that corner," and Louey felt the blood drain from her face.

"There's a cop right there," said Mia, steely. "Want me to go get him?" The girl gave Mia a cold stare, then jerked her arm away and walked on with her friends.

Around them, people stared at Louey as if she'd made a drunken scene; before she knew it, tears were streaming down her face. "Sweetheart." Mia took her in her arms.

. . .

"Do you like it?" Two days later Mia stood framed in the doorway of a new apartment as far away from their now tainted neighborhood as she could find. No one did that, Louey wanted to explain, just walked around New York as if it were a friendly five-and-dime and found a closet, much less a sunny, big apartment in a lovely neighborhood. No one but someone for whom "Sorry, we can't help you" was as alien a phrase as "Face reality, why don't you?"

"Well?" Mia prodded. Louey walked several timid steps inside and looked around; her heart felt as if it might fly out of her chest. And Mia hadn't even let on what she'd planned. How had she ever found someone so wonderful? "No, no, no, miss," the narrator's disdainful voice was sure to break in any minute. "That was Mr. Kennedy's order. Yours is over here."

"Love what you've done with the place." She turned from the window, where a view of trees and grass soothed her eyes. "When do we move in?"

"Today. It's ours." Mia looked at her with such affection Louey wondered how she'd come to deserve this happiness. "There's even room for the children."

"Honey, there's something I've been meaning to tell you."

"Can it wait until I've reduced you to a helpless wreck?" Mia flung her arms around her, collapsing them both on the floor.

"You're insane," said Louey as Mia kissed her: bullet-fast kisses that weakened her until she lay back, out of breath and wanting more. Yet she was obviously the one who was crazy, taking all this as a matter of course. "I can't believe you did this just for me."

"Heavens! Did I say *you*? I don't know *what* I could have been thinking." Mia bent and kissed her, not coming up for air. "The property values are certain to go up, of course," she added, reaching to undo Louey's dress. "Once the neighbors see what I've got, they'll all want one."

The day after she'd brought the pile of boxes back to her apartment, Louey walked around the city, looking at tall buildings as if she'd never seen Fifth Avenue before, St. Patrick's Cathedral, the Plaza Hotel. At Forty-second Street she walked east to the public library, sitting on the steps among the crowd of people. After an existential juggler tried to draw her out, she rose and made her way back home.

In the evening, she walked all the way across town to a quiet, winding street she hadn't visited in years. "I'm telling you she'll do it," warned a woman standing at the door as Louey reached her destination.

"She's *always* doing that," said Louey, entering the bar.

"See?" the woman told her friend, whose face went slack, surprised at Louey's boldness. "It's hopeless. Tell her." She nudged Louey, who smiled faintly, moving toward the bartender.

A feline woman sang on monitors up near the ceiling in the inner room, and Louey watched her, mesmerized. The bar was just as she remembered, light wood with tall stools, although the video jukebox was new. "What do you need, sugar?" asked a Nordic woman sitting at the bar. Louey told her, putting down a minor fortune for her drink.

"Amazing," she said, half to herself. The seated woman, who was angular but pretty, glanced at her questioningly. "I remember when it used to take about a month to get a drink."

"Depends on who you know." The woman lightly stroked her arm. My, *that* was fast, thought Louey, moving to the inner room.

"Any chance that I can steal this stool?" she asked a pretty blond girl, who turned out to be a boy. She couldn't remember the last time she'd seen a male in a women's bar; what, she thought, was the world coming to?

"You can borrow it until my boyfriend tears himself out of the bathroom." She must have looked uncertain, because the boy added, "Go ahead, it usually takes hours."

Louey sat and glanced around the noisy room. There seemed to be a wealth of boys, she noticed, absorbed in animated conversation with women who were far prettier than she remembered women in bars being. Designer lesbians: for once she was in the minority not wearing makeup. The blond man smiled at her. "Are they nice to boys here?" she said.

He shrugged. "Depends." One of the people in his group, a black woman with a lilting accent, glanced at Louey.

"I've brought male friends here," she said, "and they've been asked to leave as soon as they don't have a drink in their hands." She shrugged; the woman to her left, a sweet-faced girl with shoulder-length fine hair, leaned to her, whispering something in her ear. The first girl nodded, patting her friend on the back, then turned to Louey. "Need another drink?"

"I'm fine, thanks." Louey toasted with her half-full glass. The black woman left for the bar.

"I'm Belle," the second girl said. "That was Leo."

"As in—?"

"Leonie." Even the names had taken on character since she'd last been here.

Leonie came back a moment later, muttering. "This town's filled with heartless women, break you into pieces much as look at you."

"Leo likes to talk like dime-store novels when she's had too much to drink," her friend explained.

"Since when is nine drinks too many?"

"Nine?" Louey stared.

"Lying through her teeth," Belle mentioned.

When Louey had partaken of as much alcohol, smoke and conversation as she could manage, she rose, staggering.

"Need a ride?" Belle asked. "Wait till you see my car— it's gorgeous."

"You have a car?"

Belle laughed at Louey's tone and put an arm around her. "I'll drive you home," she said.

They walked out into the night air, Louey incredulous that she was in this sudden fix. At her building, an open parking space brazenly awaited them, gleaming malevolently. "Shame to let this go to waste," Belle murmured.

"Come on up." Louey's blood was pounding in her ears; how could she have said that? Her hands shook slightly as she fit the key into the lock; she laughed, embarrassed. "Have a seat"—she let them in and motioned to the couch. "Do you want a drink? Coffee?"

"Whatever." Belle looked around the apartment, turned as Louey crossed the room to get their drinks and kissed her easily, as if she'd done it countless times before. Smiling, she let Louey go and sat down on the couch.

Louey's head was whirling. The kiss had been unhurried, skilled. ("Baby," she heard Mia's voice asking, "was that something you made up yourself?") She sat back on the couch, setting their drinks beside them. Belle ran a hand through Louey's hair, then bent to kiss her; Louey lay flat against the couch, swallowing. ("Run that by me one more time?" said Mia.)

Why was she even thinking about Mia? She closed her eyes, fighting back tears. ("Keep them open," Mia whispered.) Louey's heart battered her chest. The walls of her apartment seemed to close in on her; she felt as if her mind were somewhere far above her, looking down. Who was this lying numbly on the couch, her body smarting?

Some hours later, the phrase "I have no job" came wafting through her head. She pictured Kevin standing in her office, looking as if he were about to cry. "But what about Clay, Louey?" she could hear his plaintive voice as they went over what to do with all her authors. What *about* Clay, she thought. (Mia didn't answer.)

She doesn't love you anymore, Louey thought: why can't you face it? Soft, unfamiliar breathing filled the room, and tears stung Louey's eyes. What am I going to do? she wondered. A strange hand lay across her stomach: carefully she lifted it off and placed it on the mattress. She lay looking out the window until the sun crept over the horizon, greeting a new day.

The only reason Clay agreed over the telephone to meet Charlene was the distress he heard in her voice. Yet when he arrived at the appointed meeting place, there was no sign of her. Charlene *would* pick an overpriced pretentious joint like this, he thought, glancing around the restaurant. White plastic gleamed as far as he could see; electric-colored toys and bright-eyed waiters cluttered the horizon. His drink, when it arrived at last, was ninety per-cent water. Next time, he'd force her to a dive he favored, just to see the look on her face. If there ever was a next time.

After thirty minutes, he called for the waiter, thinking he would get himself another drink. Then he changed his mind—he could do better than these feeble cocktails—and asked the future Oscar-winning actor for his check. His pseudo-drink came to $5.70 plus tax; he left the money on the table, rising in disgust.

Just as he reached the door, Charlene breezed in. "Where are you going?" she demanded. He could barely bring him-self to answer, waving her outside. She trailed behind him, exasperated. "Clayton Lee. If you don't stop this instant, I won't take another step."

He paused, turning to her. "I can't stay here, Charlene. You should know too much good breeding makes me dizzy."

"Where do you suggest we go?"

"I don't care." He started walking; then a cool hand on his shoulder stopped him.

"Must we walk for miles?" she asked.

He hailed a cab and gave it his address, to which Charlene responded with a satisfied, thin smile. Clay stared out the window as they neared his place, then paid the driver. Charlene waited for him to extend a hand, then climbed out of the cab herself, sorely put-upon.

"So what's this grave catastrophe of yours?" he said once they were inside and he'd shed his tie.

"May I have a drink, please?" He despised that pout; no doubt in thirty years he'd still be able to describe it perfectly. Surely the world was filled with people more like Louey than like Charlene; he'd just had bad luck finding them. Fixing Charlene a Scotch, he handed her the glass and lit her outstretched cigarette obligingly. She inhaled, shaking smooth hair off her neck, and settled back as if recovering from a journey. "Well, I've just been treated wretchedly, that's all. I've been—disposed of." She eyed him as if daring him to come to her defense.

"You mean dumped?"

"Please." She took a long drink and several melodramatic puffs on her cigarette.

"Well, everyone gets dumped, Charlene. You even dumped me, remember?"

"Clayton." She shook her head. "I thought we'd put all that behind us. You should be over me by now."

He laughed. "You're right, Charlene, I should be—and guess what? I am. Now what has this got to do with your big problem? You were nearly hysterical on the phone."

"You don't think it means anything that someone I've been dating for two years should up and discard me like an old mink coat?"

Heightened emotion made her face quite vivid, prettier than usual. How could someone so lovely be so dull? "Well, it's a jungle out there, Char." He downed his drink and made himself another. "So that's the reason for the call, to tell me this?"

"As if it weren't enough," she sniffed. "You'd obviously prefer even worse things happen to me."

"But what's it got to do with me, Charlene? What is it you want me to do about it?" He didn't know why he'd been so stupid as to bring her here; now he would have to come up with some excuse to make her leave.

"I just don't want to be alone tonight," she said.

He stared at her. She looked at him in earnest; she couldn't see a thing wrong with what she was asking. "Charlene—"

"Now don't get all mean, not to me, tonight. I've had an awful day."

"Charlene, you can't seriously expect that after you and I have hardly spoken three words to each other over the last five years, you should snap your fingers and expect me to—"

"Clay, I'm very unhappy." A tear coursed down her cheek; she had no shame. This was too much. "Please, Clay, just let me stay with you tonight."

"No." He turned to make another drink, and she rose off the couch, draping herself around him from behind and licking his ear. "Jesus!" He moved away, angry to find himself responding even slightly. "Cut it out!"

"You're lonely, too," she said. "I can tell. And you know we were always good together." She swept her hand across the front of him, brushing his crotch; he flung himself across the room, eyes blazing.

"Cut it out *now*, Charlene." He knew he looked insane; this was ridiculous. He didn't want her shallow, mindless self. "Go home and find yourself another nursemaid."

"I know you want to." She smiled, brushing a fine strand off her forehead. He tried to look menacing but couldn't hide or will away his arousal, looming like part of some completely unrelated body. He felt only contempt for her, but her caresses had been sure; she knew his body better than her own, and it had been too long since anyone had touched him.

"Give me a break, Charlene," he said. "I'm not a robot, but I'm not about to sleep with you. It's very sad your boyfriend dumped you, but you can't stay here. I don't have a thing to offer you." At the sight of her smirk, his desire subsided, happily, and he regained a grip on his emotions. "Be reasonable, honey, you'll find someone else," he added more gently. He turned to put her glass in the sink. Before he knew it, she was kneeling at his feet, her arms around his legs. He was mortified. "Jesus, Charlene, pull yourself together." He tried to raise her to her feet, but she went slack. Then, when he bent to help her, she unzipped his pants and reached inside. Before it had dawned on him what she was doing, she had taken him into her mouth. "Christ—!" he swore, and tried to extricate himself, but she soon followed, expert as she'd always been. To catch his breath, he leaned against the sink; then, looking at her, he felt his will evaporate. It was hopeless. He would pay for this, he knew. Louey's face came floating before his eyes and he knocked Charlene's head against him in self-loathing and excitement. Then he came, despairing, and covered his face. The last thing he wanted was to spend another minute with this woman. But as she rose, brushing her breasts against the front of him, he knew he would do everything she asked.

After not quite a month of Charlene, vermouth, and a hint of lime, Clay decided it was time to start looking for a woman he could enjoy while sober. The perfection of Charlene's body only emphasized the emptiness it encased; she'd been a fitting complement to his post-Louey phase, but once he snapped out of his minor coma, he had no excuse to keep seeing her.

To his surprise, meeting new people turned out to be far easier than he'd expected. Soon he was socializing with a vengeance. One immediate result of this was pure poetic justice: Charlene met somebody at a party they attended and left Clay for him. Now all he had to do was find someone to take his mind off Louey.

He often thought of calling her, but never got past picking up the phone. What would be the point? Even if she conceded that the situation had been stupid all around, she'd never care for or desire him. What had prompted him to choose such an unlikely object for his affection? He must be insane.

One day he got a letter from her office, followed by a pile of revised pages from his manuscript, which Kevin had discovered cleaning out her desk. He couldn't believe she'd left her job! Well, that took care of that, he thought; she'd quit and hadn't even tried to call him. There went the lingering possibility of getting his book finished, much less published: *Bright Lights, Dead Pussy*, he thought grimly. What if they'd had a formal contract, he wondered, instead of just the hope of one? He flipped through several sections, catching glimpses of her scrawl, and had to put the pages back inside the box, the force of his reaction startling him. He poured himself a Scotch, toasting the now-defunct manuscript, but put the glass down without touching it, his hands shaking slightly. In a sudden burst of inspiration, he emptied the trash can next to his typewriter and lit a sheet, igniting the pile of manuscript pages with a feeling of perverse satisfaction at the theatricality of his gesture.

The next week he went out and got himself a job playing piano at a quirky late-night restaurant. This was easy: he could be like every other trendy pseudo-artist in Manhattan, he thought. Playing gave him pleasure, but though strangers spoke to him easily and often, he could hardly bring himself to see them as potential lovers, friends, companions. Night after night he let music enfold him. It was a strange relief to feel so empty, unattached.

The depths to which he'd sunk became apparent when Clay found himself accepting dinner at his father's house. Although he sensed a setup in the making, he could hardly bring himself to care. Sure enough, his stepmother opened the door (his father had never seemed to feel the need to open a door in his life) and steered him toward a tall, dark, handsome woman, who took his hand in greeting. Her name was Brooke, it turned out, and she was an associate at his father's firm. She was intelligent, he had to give his father credit—as substantial as Charlene was frivolous. He almost enjoyed talking with her (despite the gleam in his father's eye), but though felt himself responding to her charm, he couldn't imagine spending time alone with her.

So many men and women his own age seemed wholly without whimsy, he'd discovered, so unswerving in the pursuit of goals that it was hard to picture their ever having been children. His father alluded to his future—giving up the vagabond's life, a brief foray at law school, and then instant partnership—but for once he didn't press, no doubt owing to the presence of his lovely guest.

After several hours of dining pleasure, Clay wondered how to end the evening; he was clearly expected to squire Brooke home, or at least to ask her out, a prospect he didn't view with much enthusiasm. He was being rude to her, he knew. He was equally unfair to women whom he met at work, at parties: nice ones, women smart enough to be involved with, but never anyone he could feel inclined to see again. It didn't seem quite right to waste the time of some nice, normal person when all he really wanted was to be with one small oddball. See you later, Pops, he thought. Bidding an abrupt good night, he ignored Clayton's obvious displeasure at his failure to take conclusive action. Sorry, I've got to go home and carry a torch for a dyke, he thought as Brooke smoothly got her things and left with him. As they rode the elevator in silence, he strained to think of something light to put her off. She surprised him, saying, "My car's outside. I'll drop you."

Who had a car in New York City? he thought, falling in beside her. Her decisiveness was impressive; he was almost curious to see what she would do with him.

Instead of asking where he lived, she drove him to her place—luxurious and immaculately furnished, he soon learned. Why he'd been silent, simply following her lead, he couldn't say. As long as there were women to take charge of things, he supposed he'd never have to make a move. Was this the way the world worked, really—was the notion that men were the ones in charge pure myth?

Impassively he watched as she made drinks, then slipped

out of her clothes as casually as if she were preparing for a bath in total solitude. He took in the well-formed body as he sipped his drink. She sat down next to him, kissing his neck, then worked the buttons of his shirt with expert hands. (He felt as if he were some large device she was employing for her own release.) Surely they could do better than this, he thought, and willed himself to fondle her, caressing her smooth skin (though in truth he felt more genuine enthusiasm for the drink set to one side of her). Rising slightly off the couch, he let her slip his pants off, brushing her shoulders as her hands moved across him smoothly. Finally she lowered herself onto him. Hearing himself cry out, he put his arms around her, stroking her cool back. The sound of her soft breathing echoed in his ears as she moved over him. Whatever they were doing seemed to go on for a very long time.

The next day Clay walked across the Brooklyn Bridge at dawn, watching the skyline of the city change. So many people were awake early he felt as if he'd happened upon another universe, one that went on all around him as he splashed about in a tiny corner like a child, oblivious. The air was hushed and slightly damp; his feet protested slightly as he walked through Brooklyn Heights until he reached the Promenade.

He sat down on a bench as joggers passed and women in Reeboks and business suits walked dogs. Putting down his things, he gazed across the water at the view of downtown Manhattan, serenely beautiful in the morning light.

I hate Louey, he thought suddenly. He couldn't fathom her complete abandonment of him; it didn't seem within her nature.

A group of teenage girls ogled him. He sighed: he'd write a wry, insulting letter; that would do the trick. Yawning, he rose and made his way down to the subway. "Dear Heartless Bitch"—no, that was far too understated. He'd show her he wasn't some lump who pined for women with no use for him—no matter what their sexual persuasion.

"Sincerely and with tragically misplaced affection," he thought, getting on a train.

Changing his clothes, Clay ran around the reservoir in Central Park, gritting his teeth each time a woman passed him. He should be in better shape than this, he thought; and why should women passing him make him feel so inferior? No doubt it meant deep down he thought he should be better than they were at whatever he might do. Another flaw, he thought—offending people right and left. A gay man eyed him curiously, as if he'd spoken. Clay thought of asking for advice about this lesbian he knew, but luckily the man had passed before he had the chance.

After half an hour he gave up, hobbling away from the energetic horde. He should go and work on his book, but he was damned if he could bring himself to write when Louey couldn't even get herself to speak his name. He threw himself down on a park bench, next to someone's grandmother. After several moments, he began to notice that the conversation she was having was with him. "I'm sure your children love you," he said once she'd mentioned what was troubling her.

"Young people," she went on, "all they think about today is making money. Selfish." She sighed loudly, watching several teenage boys in running gear pass, arguing. "What do you do for a living?"

I'm the coroner, he nearly said. "I'm a musician." Where had that come from?

"I was a singer when I was a girl." He stared at her. "Before the Nazis came." She clucked her tongue.

Clay thought of how he'd heard his father tell his mother he wouldn't be a Jew "for all the money in the world." (It had seemed odd to Clay, as if it were a fate something as simple as money could arrange.) His father hated everyone, he'd realized early on: poor people, women, men "who might as well be women," "niggers." (The word still made Clay's chest tight, as it had when he was a boy, though at the time he hadn't quite known why.) How could someone like that be his father? he'd thought. What if he grew up to be just like him?

"At least in New York City people let each other be," he mentioned to the woman. In New York you could walk down any street and hear ten different languages, not one of them English. Black faces mixed with Asian, Latin, white ones from around the globe. It was a marvel—where else could the product of so many different lands mix in one place?

"The blacks, they hate the Jews," the woman said. "The Puerto Ricans hate the black ones, too."

"Not everyone." It pained Clay when he came upon dissension among people he had hoped would be more sensitive than he. Well, he had one small problem now himself: gay people.

"Ach, America." The woman gazed off into the distance, and Clay looked with her.

When he'd met Mia years ago, he'd started noticing gay men—gay women were far harder to pick out—somehow both intrigued and put off by the air of insulation they projected, angry self-protection, proud defiance. When he'd gotten to know Louey, some of the strangeness had worn off: her world seemed private, magical, a family that lived underground but snuck out every night to play. He'd almost envied her for being different, even for having to fight to prove what she was.

Now suddenly he found himself consumed with hatred for the very thing he had admired. Why the fuck did she have to be gay; why couldn't she want him, like other women? Would it have killed her? Would loving him have been so goddamned horrible?

He had nothing to be proud of, he knew that: his lordly,

stupidly oblivious background, his shiftless life. He hated the intolerance that had overtaken him, as if before his very eyes he was fulfilling his worst fears, turning into his father. He remembered fleetingly how he'd once wanted to be black; it seemed ironic now.

Well, he loved her. He thought about the friend he'd laughed with, teased, and fallen for, though surely all the physical insanity would soon have passed. He loved her. Even as he clung to newfound bigotry as if his life depended on it, it made him happy just to think of something she had said, some teasing, silly conversation. He loved her: it was the worst thing he had ever done.

After a shower and some hours of lying on his bed composing letters, Clay went down to get his mail. Along with several bills and six requests for money was a postcard of a surly, nude young man whose name appeared to be "Kept Boy." Next to his blond head was the caption: " 'Not another goddamned Mercedes,' he whined."

Clay turned it over, feeling slightly dizzy. "Glad to hear the wife's hair is beginning to grow back after that nasty lederhosen incident," he read. "Too bad you couldn't both have been here for the firing." He blinked, feeling a strange sensation in his chest. "Hope you're hard at work. (Any chance I can get you to rewrite the character of the bitch editor your hero murders? I know, wishful thinking.) Miss your tawdry face. Best to the little ones." Clay stood in the middle of his lobby, staring at the card until the doorman came and asked if there was anything he wanted.

"No," he said. Nothing worth mentioning.

Louey unpacked the last of her boxes, filling one corner of the shelves in the small office. Taking a folder from the pile across her desk, she began to hang up photographs and cartoons to give the room a warmer, lived-in look. In the midst of hanging up a poster, she heard a sound and looked down from the chair she was standing on to see the smiling face of her new boss. She started to step down.

"No, go on with what you're doing," the woman stopped her. Gloria was nearly as young as she was, tanned from a business trip out West. "I see you're making yourself at home," she went on. "We're glad you're here."

"Thank you." Louey smiled at her. It was odd not having to be tense whenever her boss came into a room. At this new office, everyone was friendly, casual.

"Agents have been calling to tell me what a catch we got," Gloria added, handing her a pushpin.

"They live to flatter."

"They think they're telling me something I don't know." She shook her head. "Well, give a holler if you need anything I haven't thought of. The phones should be connected by tomorrow; your business cards will take a little longer."

"Thanks." But tell me, she wanted to ask, when is this elated mood of mine going to fade?

She'd met the editor in chief of one of the few existing civilized publishing houses at a dinner party that an agent friend had thrown; to her surprise, Gloria was not only smart and sane, she even liked Louey. Louey went through the next weeks in shock: she was being courted by a reputable publisher, she might even get a decent job! The thought was overwhelming.

"Well?" Kevin had asked just two weeks earlier at Lincoln Center. "How's freedom?"

"Everyone keeps telling me how half of publishing's been fired." She sat down by the fountain. "But secretly I know they all think I deserved it." She'd never known how powerless, how utterly defeated, she could feel—as if she had to prove her competence to everyone. "I wouldn't have gotten fired if it hadn't been for . . ."

"Your overweening tastefulness?" He sat down next to her. "Your authors are going out of their minds, I have to tell you." He swung his legs against the ledge of the fountain. "It would have helped if you'd let on what life was really like at Regent—if only you'd been less discreet."

"It's always been a problem of mine."

He beat his fists together. "It's horrible without you, Louey. I'm taking my vacation as soon as possible." He took a breath. "And they promoted me."

"Kevin!" She grabbed his arm. "That's wonderful! At least now you won't be at the beck and call of some cheap floozy."

"I was worried they'd give me a straight man."

"They wouldn't *dare.*" She gazed into the foamy water, shielding her eyes. "I'm so glad my authors have you taking care of them."

"You aren't mad?" She stared, then put an arm around his shoulders. "Then you don't mind if I put pictures of naked boys on all the covers, right?" He ducked a punch. "Just testing." He took a deep breath. "So . . ."

She waited. "What?" He wouldn't meet her eye. "What, Kevin?"

"It's . . ." He watched a stream of overdressed young concertgoers pass. "Have you called Clay?"

She still could feel the cool hand on her shoulder as she'd turned to find him standing in her office on the verge of tears her last day.

"Every time I tried to mention him—"

"I went into a coma." She sighed. "I just keep seeing—"

"Louey." He covered her hand. "It's not his fault."

"I wrote him." She studied her feet. "But I can't bring myself to call him. What would I say: Hi, Clay—I'm so sorry about wanting you wiped from the planet, can we be friends a century from now, once I've forgotten how to spell Mia's name?"

"That's v-i-x-e-n."

"And what if I don't get a job? I won't be much good to him then." She blinked. "Or anybody."

"I won't listen to such talk."

The thought of never working on a book again was too painful to bear. She rose to her feet. "Do you think a girl could get arrested just for leaping into the fountain?"

"What's that got to do with you?"

She laughed, striking a pose as if preparing for a dive. "I know one way to find out . . ."

He took her outstretched hand. "Going somewhere?" He squeezed hard. She smiled, starting to slip her hand from his, but he wouldn't let go. "Without me?" he asked, holding fast.

Several weeks at her new office increased Louey's elation; rather than confirming her worst fears, she learned there was a decent way to work. For the first time she looked forward to going to the office, going out with agents, authors. This was what it really meant to be an editor: to help books come to life. It was as if she had been freed from prison. She never dreamed she'd get to work with people she respected, people she could learn from, even *like*. It was a miracle.

Clay's unfinished manuscript lay unopened in a corner of her office. She tried to call, but each time she picked up the phone she saw the shame contort his face as he looked first at Mia and then at her. The postcard had been faceless; talking to his voice seemed utterly impossible. Nor had Clay had the nerve to call her, either—though nearly the day after she'd mailed the card, she had gotten a note wishing her good luck finding a job. Now chances were he wouldn't even finish working on his book. No, that was silly; surely he'd have found another publisher by now, an editor impressed by his connections, soaking up his charm. He *was* charming, she thought. Still, there was something that kept Clay from seeming smug or arrogant like other pretty, rich boys.

Odd that she hadn't run into him walking down the street. Well, maybe not so odd; he took cabs everywhere—a cab for every mile she walked.

Her phone rang, startling her. She answered, cheerfully greeting a new author. In a minute she had turned from Clay's manuscript and soon forgotten all but the work at hand.

"Is this the most fabulous brother the world has ever known?" Louey put her pencil down, surprised.

"Hello? Hello?" He tapped the phone. "Mr. de Mille?"

"I'm ready for my close-up."

"Is this my retarded baby sister?"

"John-John?" She hadn't heard his voice in years, it seemed. She straightened several papers on her desk. "How are you, Danny?"

"Who wants to know?"

"Peachy," she said, "that's how I am, if you *must* know. How was your trip?"

"Endless. But enough about you. What are you doing to prepare for my imminent visit?"

"When?"

"Friday. And I'm bringing someone, so you'd better mind your manners."

"Someone? Is this a mystery sweetheart? A biological twin? No one told me."

"Afraid you'd embarrass yourself, as usual."

"Who's calling, please?"

"I met her in—no, that was someone else. Japan, I think—

or was it Guam? Her name is Carole. You'll love her. Just don't drool all over her in gratitude."

"She gets more than enough of that from you, I bet."

Friday arrived and he appeared at seven on the dot, a sweet-faced Asian woman in tow. Carole seemed to thrive on giving Danny a hard time, which instantly endeared her to his sister.

After a dinner that left them all slightly dazed with over-indulgence, her brother's girlfriend insisted on going out to get dessert. Brother and sister lay inert on the floor as Carole bustled out of the apartment.

"She's wonderful." Louey raised herself on one elbow. "How much are you paying her?"

"Millions," he said fondly. "You should have one of your own, you know. Seeing anyone?"

Her stomach lurched. "No," she said, swallowing. "No one since—"

Silence hung in the air for a moment, until her brother rose from the floor and plopped himself on the couch.

"Since—?" he prompted.

"Since Mia," she managed, watching his face.

He studied her calmly; as far as she could tell, his expression hadn't changed. "I was wondering if you'd ever tell me."

"I didn't think—"

"I'd understand? Louey." He shook his head. "I want you to be happy, girl."

"You do?" She was suddenly on the verge of tears, it seemed. Danny raised a hand as if to stop the flow, which finished her. She covered her brimming eyes.

He put an arm around her shoulders, caressing her hair. "You okay?"

"I just—" She tried to stop her eyes from spilling over. "I just wish I could get over her."

"You deserve better."

"It doesn't exist."

"Why? Because she was beautiful? Because she didn't know a good thing enough to hold on to it?"

"She loved me."

"Honey—" He tightened his hold. "Mia wasn't in full control of her own emotions, much less anyone else's. She certainly wasn't capable of giving you real love."

"How do you know?"

He sighed. "Sweetheart, I saw her with you all those years. You were like her—her toy, something she used to brighten up her days. The two of you acted like children, oblivious to the rest of the world."

"Isn't that what being in love is?"

"But it wasn't the same for her. She loved being with you, I'm not saying she didn't, but she was barely capable of taking care of herself, much less being there for someone else. And there you were, willing to give up anything for her. She just didn't deserve it."

"I think she did." At this the buzzer rang, and Danny got up to let Carole in. Her arms were full. Louey rose to take out dishes for dessert.

"Louey, why did you break up?" her brother said. His girlfriend glanced at him.

"I don't know." She bit her lip, holding back another outbreak of sobs.

He came up behind her, putting his hands on her shoulders. "Do you think it's fair that after all you meant to each other, one day she could just say hit the road and that was that, no explanation necessary?" She shrugged; he shook her gently. "I'm not saying Mia meant to hurt you, I think she was just scared by how deeply you felt. I think that maybe what you had together wasn't what you thought it was. You were so innocent, you know. Your first time in love—"

"What makes you say that?"

"Don't be a dope." He took a dish of ice cream from Carole's hands. "I'm your brother, I know these things. Maybe it was just physical. Maybe it wasn't really love."

"We were friends for a long time first."

"You were something, but I don't know if it was friends. You were under each other's spell. But there was always something vaguely unnatural about it." He grimaced, stopping her objection. "I don't mean that way. There was just this possessed quality about you both, this hypercharged air when you were together, as if you turned into completely different people."

"Unlike lizard-face and me," Carole interjected.

"Right," he agreed. "Now we're as boring as two old flannel shirts. We couldn't be on good behavior with each other if we tried."

"Well, that's wonderful for you two," Louey said, "but not everyone experiences love that way."

"More's the pity." He took Carole in his arms, giving her a squeeze. She swatted him on the nose.

"Ratbag," she said affectionately. "Now isn't it time we all see how fat we can get?" She poised her spoon and beamed at Louey, looking so angelic Louey had no choice but to obey.

After they had left, Louey lay awake and listened to the music on the street, accompanied by the sound of car alarms. It amazed her that her brother had such strong opinions on a subject she'd thought he'd been utterly oblivious about. Imagine his not feeling anything but love for her. She pulled the covers tightly around her. Imagine thinking Mia wasn't good enough for her, she marveled, dropping off to sleep.

The next day Louey walked into her office only to find her phone ringing insistently. I haven't even taken off my *shoes*, she thought, picking up the receiver. "Hello?"

"Louey?"

"Is this my favorite art director?" No sooner had she greeted the familiar voice from her former office than Louey heard such unexpected news her heart stopped. Dead: Kevin was dead? He couldn't be. Her friend had insufficient details to prevent the phrase from echoing mindlessly: Kevin dead? She hung up finally, bolting to the bathroom.

The publicity director stood before the mirror, toying with her hair. "You all right?" she asked, seeing Louey's face.

"I just heard some bad news." Louey stood by the sink uncertainly. At last the woman left, and Louey stared into the mirror.

"Better now?" Later in the day, she looked up to see the publicity director in her doorway. Better? thought Louey, nodding. She stared at the pages on her desk, wondering why they usually seemed to have meaning. What else mattered but that he was suddenly, forever, without warning, gone?

The next few weeks she went around the office in a daze.

Her friends both in and out of work quickly found out what had happened, but they seemed bewildered that she was so shaken by it, so unable to smile or come up with her usual sarcastic quips. She couldn't read or sleep; she couldn't seem to do much of anything. Surely her shock would fade, she thought. It had to lift eventually. Yet each new day she felt as shaken and bewildered as before.

She'd been barely ten the day her mother told her that her father wouldn't be returning from the hospital where he'd been for several weeks; she hadn't cried then, certain that she'd see him soon—why on earth was everyone acting so strange about it? She'd been lucky, she saw now, to lose a father at so young an age, before she'd known what she was truly losing. Now, years later, she was suddenly consumed with fear—her mother could die as abruptly as he had; her brothers—*anyone*. She felt so paralyzed she wondered if she'd ever make it through a night without awakening in tears.

Clay was in the Village late one evening when he saw her walking down the street across from him, an odd expression on her face. He felt almost ill, seeing her so unexpectedly. Hurrying to make the light, he called her name. She didn't answer. He rushed to catch up with her, placing himself directly in her path. She looked at him blankly, moving to step past him.

"Louey?" he said, reaching out to take her arm. Something must be terribly wrong: she stared as if she'd never seen him before. "Are you all right?"

"Clay." She spoke his name in amazement, as if she'd forgotten he existed. "I'm—" To his surprise, her eyes filled.

"Louey"—he clutched her arm—"what is it?"

"It's—Kevin died." At this, she turned a crumpled face away from him, dissolving into tears.

"You can't—what happened?"

She told him, haltingly, as a new outburst overtook her. Before he knew what he was doing, he had taken her in his arms. She was damp and warm, and he tightened his hold on her. Every tremor pierced his body. What if he never let her go?

"When did it happen?"

"A month ago." She moved out of his arms at last, turning a blotched face up to him. "I still wake up each morning thinking he's alive, before it dawns on me." She wiped her face, hands trembling, and explained that Kevin had gone on vacation, "to celebrate his promotion." Her eyes rounded, glistening. "On the way to his parents' house, a drunken driver hit his car, killing him instantly. I can't believe it," she murmured. "I just know he's still alive."

"I wish he were." He hooked his arm through hers.

"I keep thinking it'll stop bothering me so much."

"You can't expect to put it out of your mind just like that." He led her a few steps. "I was going to get a drink— will you come with me?"

"Well . . ."

"Come on, what were you planning on doing, just walking around aimlessly, hoping to get hit by a car yourself?" He tightened his hold on her, chilled by his words. She seemed so fragile suddenly.

"Okay," she said at last. "Sure you don't mind?"

"Don't be insane. I'd rather be with you than anyone in the world."

She blinked, trying to smile. "So how have you been? I've been meaning to call you."

"I've been okay. I wish you had called me about Kevin."

"I know. I've been trying to stop thinking about it. Everyone around the office keeps looking at me strangely, like, Oh, that, aren't you over it yet?"

"People just don't know how to react. I'm sure they're concerned for you."

"It's the most amazing thing. It's as if my friends are embarrassed for me."

They reached the bar. "Try not to take it personally." He steered her to a dark corner. "Death makes everyone uncomfortable." He ordered drinks, sitting down across from her. How strange it was to see her under these conditions, looking so lost.

"Do you know," she said, "you were the only person who just put your arms around me? All my other friends just stood by, looking uncomfortable."

"They don't know how to react."

"But you did."

He took a drink, wanting to brush the hair away from her flushed face. It was true that for months he'd longed to take her in his arms, but seeing her so wretched he'd just acted, wanting only to console her. "I liked him, too, you know."

"He was—" She ran a finger down the surface of her glass, tears threatening again. "He was such a joy to have around. God, he used to—he could always make me laugh. Sometimes it seemed as if he'd love me no matter what I did."

"I'm sure he wasn't the only one of your friends who feels that way, Louey." This was too close to a confession of his own, too tawdry, and he swallowed, emptying his glass.

"Sometimes I think he was the only one." She tilted her head back as if she were drinking water.

"Easy. You don't want to get sick."

"Why not?" She motioned for another round. "This must be great fun for you, watching me cry."

"I just want you to be happy, Louey."

She was silent, playing with her straw. "That's what my brother said."

"Hasn't your family been any help to you?"

"They don't understand why I'm taking it so hard; he's

not family, after all." She laughed joylessly. "I think they're offended that I should care so much about a stranger."

"I'm sure it's hard for them to see you in such pain."

"You, on the other hand, must be used to it by now. First Mia and now Kevin. What a swell date."

"The worst." He squeezed her hand as she talked on and drank as if completely unaffected by the alcohol. It was so strange just sitting here with her, a miracle his presence could help at all.

Without warning, her eyelids began to droop: she was on the verge of passing out, he realized. He didn't know why he was sober himself. Taking her hand, he led her to the street and hailed a cab. After they got in, she nestled drowsily against his shoulder, falling asleep. It stung his eyes, though he felt happier than he'd thought possible. At his apartment, he lifted her easily in his arms—she was so tiny!—and carried her upstairs. His apartment was warm; he struggled briefly with his conscience, then deposited her on the bed and stripped the pants from her dispassionately. Finding an oversized T-shirt for her, he unbuttoned her shirt, averting his eyes as he slipped the T-shirt over her and pulled the other off. Before he went to make the couch up, he sat for just a minute in the chair across from her, studying her sleeping face. Why should the sight of her curled up against his pillow fill him with such happiness? He couldn't get up from the chair for fear it was the last time he would ever get to feel this way.

When Louey woke up, she saw Clay sprawled out on a chair across from her, half sitting, half lying. His hand hung over the side of the chair's arm, his mouth half open, shoulders posed as if he'd fallen asleep in the middle of a shrug. Even in that position he looked comfortable, and Louey wished that she could be as carefree and at ease as he was, blanking out without a second thought.

His legs were bare and tanned in shorts, covered with golden fuzz. She sat up slightly, pulling the covers up over her bare legs. She seemed to be wearing an unfamiliar T-shirt, and she blushed at the realization that he must have undressed her and put it on. Her clothes lay neatly folded on the table next to his chair; his shirt lay crumpled on the floor at his feet. Clay's chest was almost that of a little boy's, honey-colored like his legs, the tan slightly deeper at the belly, which was flat and lightly muscled. A small patch of golden hair on his chest and near the top of his shorts was the only indication that he wasn't still a boy. She felt an odd affection for his boy's body, reminded of her brothers' healthy, buoyant frames. A pang of nostalgia for the comfort of their arms slung casually around her shoulders struck her.

As if conscious of her examination of him, Clay opened his eyes and Louey found herself staring into them. He seemed still half asleep as he held her gaze, scratching his chest and then letting his arm fall into his lap. The palm faced up, like an invitation, and Louey saw that the front of his shorts was full. It was an odd sensation being here with him, somehow so intimately; as Louey examined him curiously, his face flushed, making him look even more like a sleepy little boy caught in the act of doing something naughty, ripe and lush. She looked at the parted lips and wondered if women enjoyed kissing him. As if he'd read her mind, his skin turned a deeper rose and he shivered, sitting up and clearing his throat.

"You sleep all right?" he asked, shifting uneasily and trying casually to clench his fists together in his lap.

"Better than you, I'll bet." He was embarrassed, she realized. "I didn't mean for you to give up your own bed."

"Don't be silly," he said. "I can sleep anyplace." He cleared his throat. "Would you like some breakfast?"

"I should get dressed and get out of your hair." Though the prospect of going home held little appeal, she hated to impose on him further.

"Please don't go, Louey," he said softly, lowering his eyes. His face grew inexplicably sad, and when he raised his eyes, she saw with astonishment that he was blinking back tears.

"Why, Clay, whatever is the matter?" she asked, alarmed.

He shrugged, looking irritated. "Don't mind me, I'm just hung over." Abruptly he left her; a moment later Louey heard him making coffee. "Do you drink coffee?" he called out.

"Tea?"

"Sure. Anything for breakfast? Eggs? Squid?"

"How about some lithium?"

A pause followed, and Louey smelled the aroma of fresh coffee brewing. "Seem to be all out, sorry. Should have been here yesterday."

"I was, apparently."

He came in a few minutes later with a mug of tea, sitting down beside her on the bed. He had put on a clean shirt, which made him look slightly more presentable.

"I guess I spilled my guts, huh?"

"I don't mind." He took a drink and she watched his Adam's apple bob up and down as he swallowed. Men had such strange bodies. "You can't keep those things bottled up inside you, you know."

"I suppose." She sniffed her mug and screwed up her nose. "What did you put in here?"

"You did want tea, didn't you?" He looked altogether too innocent.

"What else is in here?"

"Just a little something." He drank his coffee impassively. "Rum."

"For breakfast?"

"Some days nothing else will do." His tone was emphatic. "Now listen to your mother and drink up."

She had to admit the hot alcohol made her feel better. She hadn't slept in weeks, it seemed, until last night. She should feel ashamed of her loss of control the night before, she knew, but somehow she wasn't. "This is great. Just what I needed."

"See?"

"You're very sweet to take care of me."

He looked away, suddenly red-faced. "You'd do the same for any anonymous wandering city girl."

"Well . . ."

"I missed you, you know." He punched her shoulder lightly. "After all you've done for me, this is the least I can do."

"I don't know what I would have done without you yesterday, Clay." She sipped her tea, for the first time able to think about Kevin almost calmly.

"I'm glad you trusted me."

"I'm sorry I didn't call you after I was fired. I've been meaning to, you know."

"Really?" He cursed the eagerness in his voice. "The card was—special, anyway." She smiled. "I would have called, but I thought—"

"I'd still blame you for the party?"

He nodded.

"It all seems so long ago. I can't imagine why I acted so deranged. Nothing like having someone die to put things in real perspective, I guess. Everything seems so trivial compared to losing someone so—so finally." She sighed. "At least now I know I'm not shallow."

"Shallow—that's something to aim for." He sipped his coffee. "Have you thought about going away for a while? You should take some time off."

"I can't leave my new job—I've only been there a few months."

"Have you taken any time off since it happened?" She shook her head. "Do they let you take personal days?" She nodded. "Jesus, Louey, you can't expect to function as if nothing has happened. Go to your mother's, why don't you?"

"I can't face going home. My mother will just worry."

"By yourself, then?"

"I don't know what good having more time to think about it would do."

"Would you like me to take you somewhere?" He was struck with an idea. "I was thinking of renting a car and driving to my mother's—she's been nagging me to visit her ever since I convinced her I wasn't moving back home. There's a long weekend coming up, so you wouldn't even have to miss too much work."

"Wouldn't it be strange bringing a total stranger?"

He thought for a moment; it was hard to know how his mother would react. "She'd love you." He wondered if this was true. "How about it, what do you say?"

"When are you going?"

"I haven't made definite plans—when can you get off from work?"

"How long would you be going for?"

"I don't know, a week. Is that too long?"

"I probably could get some time—they're so nice at my new office I think the boss is even worried about my health." She stopped. "Look, I can't barge in on your vacation. It's very nice of you, Clay, but I don't want to be in the way."

"You'll be amazed just how at home you'll feel ten minutes after you get there," he teased. "Things are so slow back home that after a few days you won't have the energy to come back. I'll have to call and tell them you've quit."

She was wavering. "It *would* be nice to get out of the city."

"How can you say you've lived if you've never seen the South?"

"Who says I've lived?" She looked down at herself and laughed for the first time since he'd seen her the previous evening. "All right, so this shirt says I've lived. Well, if you really think it wouldn't be a burden—"

"You haven't a chance in hell of getting out of it now, girlie." He took both of her hands and squeezed them. The prospect of having time with her after all these months made him almost light-headed. "Now don't you think it's time you took off that tacky shirt and got into something respectable?"

Louey sat in the passenger seat of the rented sports car and watched the scenery speed by as if she were part of a travelogue. How had she agreed to go away for a week with a boy she hardly even knew? Glancing at Clay's profile, she could almost convince herself she wouldn't recognize him on a dark street. Yet here she was. "Traveling in style," she muttered.

It was true that since she'd broken up with Mia Louey had altered her standards of judging people. Not that she'd found the world such an engaging place the first months after it happened. Yet after some time had passed, she'd taken a hard look at herself. "What am I going to do," she'd asked Kevin. "Never talk to anyone again? Never trust anyone, so I won't get hurt?"

"Drink heavily?" he'd suggested.

No, she thought; damned if she would let one unfortunate blow destroy her ability to get along with the rest of the world. After some months, Kevin even noted that she was throwing herself into being "outgoing with a vengeance." What she now saw could indeed be accomplished more easily with the aid of alcohol she had done then on a self-dare: at bars, parties, and on the street, she took to addressing others as if she'd known them for years. To her amazement, people responded as if it were true.

She was equally surprised at the pleasure it gave her. People were extraordinarily friendly, relaxing into banter more intimate than if she were someone who knew their failings. Her friends insisted that she would be considered a lunatic anywhere but in New York, yet the strangers who so readily told her their worst fears came from all over the globe. "New York is where people go who can't control their need to blab with people they may never see again," Kevin had said by way of explanation.

Even at work, the new approach had stood her in good stead. After giving Louey startled looks—no one expected editors to look the way she did, barely five feet tall and hardly dignified—prospective authors fell into easy rapport, surprised that it was pleasant, even comfortable, talking with an editor, after all.

Clay himself had yielded happily, though unlike most of her potential authors, he'd confessed little of a personal nature. Now she supposed she would hear so much from him that there would soon be nothing about him she didn't know; what else could one do in the country for days?

Yet he'd remained silent for most of the trip so far, playing a lavish selection of tapes. There was something about Ella Fitzgerald's voice that made one not want to clutter the air oneself, she thought, sitting back and drifting off as it grew dark.

What did she know about Clay, really? She knew he hated having been born to a family with "so obscenely much money," as he put it; that, as much as he hated his father, he feared he would turn out to be like him. Louey wanted to reassure him that such a thing simply wasn't possible (but then how did she know Clayton Senior hadn't been a sweet and charming boy himself once, turned hard with the acquisition of wealth?).

What was Clay doing with her? Most straight men didn't strike up close friendships with lesbians, unless they were either titillated or secretly gay (neither of which Clay seemed to be). Sometimes when they were out together, she would leave him briefly and on her return not recognize him for an instant as he stood, a perfect idol. Surely women (and men) must have flocked to him in droves? Yet just like Mia, Clay hated his beauty, fearing that it was the only reason people were interested in him. He never spoke about girl-friends—but then neither did she, and she knew he was curious about her and Mia. Who wouldn't be, she thought; God knows she would scarcely have believed the two of them herself.

Odd that Kevin's death had made her finally understand how pointless it was to live in the past. Perhaps she and Mia could actually have a sane talk about what had happened, she thought, maybe even put their misunderstandings to rest. She sighed as the country drifted by her window, mourning what could never be again.

Clay's mother was a fragile beauty with a talent for drawing all attention in a room to her. Here in Tennessee the country—everything—was lavish, colorful; Louey felt she'd stepped backward in time, into another world. Dulcie Lee looked so much like her son it startled Louey. Here, clearly, was where his tenderheartedness had come from, too, though Dulcie disguised her softness with a hauteur that reminded Louey of Mia's mother. She wondered if there'd been any tenderness lurking in the lovely, brittle woman who'd always seemed so dissatisfied with Mia, and with Mia's father.

"I'm so happy to meet you." Clay's mother took Louey's hand. "Clay's talked about you so much I feel you're practically a member of the family."

Clay kissed his mother, who clung to him a moment longer than she'd intended. Then she pushed him away with some embarrassment, as if her display of emotion were in fact his own childish enthusiasm. "Good to see you, Mama." He kissed her again. "You look wonderful."

"I look like the last thing," she scoffed, pleased nonetheless. Louey could see on close inspection that Dulcie Lee was older than she appeared at first glance; there were fine lines etched into her face and neck which showed when she smiled. Yet her long hair, blond and luxurious against thin shoulders, gave the illusion that she was still a girl.

After they'd washed up from the ride, Clay took Louey on a tour of the house. "I feel like Jimmy Stewart in *The Philadelphia Story*," she told him when they had explored an area several times that of the house she had grown up in.

"My Hepburn days are over, kid," Clay said. "Pick another movie."

"Did you really live in all these rooms? I would have gotten lost."

"What makes you think I didn't? I had to have some form of entertainment." His smile faded. "My mother seems so much older somehow," he murmured.

"She's so happy to see you she doesn't even mind that you dragged me along."

"As long as she knows my father hates the thought of you, you're halfway toward being her best friend."

"The thought of me? I think he hates a little more than that."

He was silent. "No," he said finally. "He doesn't know you, and there's nothing about you to hate on sight."

"The hook, the scales?"

"Half his wives had those. No, see, as long as I was working with you, he couldn't enlist me in the firm."

"Why does he want you to be a lawyer if you don't want to? Or do you really not want to?"

"I never wanted to do much of anything, Louey, if you want to know the truth—except drink." He couldn't meet her eyes. "I guess that's the sign of a true alcoholic."

"Did you ever not drink so much?" She held her breath, half afraid to hear his answer.

"When I was writing, I didn't drink at all." He smiled bitterly. "So much for stereotypes. When I was growing up,

I drank to be companionable with my mother, who, as you'll notice, has few other hobbies. I suppose I would have been embarrassed if I'd realized what was going on, but all I could see was a sort of desperate need to get away from my father, which I certainly understood."

"Wasn't he ever nice to either of you?"

"I think my parents had a brief period when they were happy together, but it ended once she became pregnant with me. She'd had a really hard delivery with my sister, which made her terrified of giving birth, and I think he lost all patience with her. By the time I was born, she told me he never wanted to touch her while she was pregnant— and once he'd forgiven her for losing her shape—as he put it—"

"Jesus."

"—she no longer could stand anything about him. She couldn't believe how he'd treated her, as if her body was the result of some vulgar overindulgence and nothing to do with him at all."

"Cold. He didn't act that way when she was pregnant with your sister?"

He shook his head, "First shot at immortality, I guess." He motioned her almost conspiratorily to a small room, where he plopped down on the bed. "This was my hideout; our housekeeper, Mona, used to live here, but some nights she'd let me stay." He hugged a pillow to his chest. "At least she loved me."

"Your mom loved you."

He stretched out, closing his eyes. "Well, sure, in her way. I never doubted that, but she was someone I took care of, as if she were the child and I was the adult, or so it seemed to me." He sat up abruptly. "I guess I should check on her. Why don't I take your stuff to the guest room?"

"Which one? There are thousands."

"I'll bet she's put you in the room across the hall from mine. Let's go see."

Sure enough, there were fresh towels and flowers in the brightly painted room across the hall from Clay's.

"Pink?" Louey snorted. "You guys trying to tell me something?"

"Coming from Mother, it's a supreme compliment. Pink is her color."

"Naturally."

"I'll see you in about ten minutes, for dinner."

She nodded. A moment later she found herself facing a strange room and more pink than she'd seen in her entire life.

The next day Clay had three surprises: one waking Louey up; one finding her engrossed in conversation with his mother; and one spending the evening with her in the water.

He woke to find the sun streaming into his room and looked out the window to see the lush countryside and a fresh, clear blue sky he'd missed so much it now struck him almost physically. Standing at the window for what seemed like hours, he finally turned from the dazzling greens and browns and roused himself to go downstairs.

His mother had few words for him as they drank morning tea, nor could he bring himself to make conversation, though it gave him a sad pleasure to look at her. Why did she seem so defeated, as if she knew she was just marking time? One of the things he'd admired most about her had been her unwillingness to give up; even her insistence that her whims be treated with the utmost deference pointed to a spirit that never capitulated. It was heartbreaking to find her so caved in, as if it all had been pretense that she'd lost the will to continue. She patted his hand fondly. He wanted to shake her, force her to come to life again.

Had it not been for Louey, upstairs, asleep, oblivious to

the wreckage awaiting her, he would have taken a drink.
Yet somehow he felt he should be as clear as possible for
Louey. Maybe it was a conceit that she needed him, but it
was one he wanted to believe.

At twelve-thirty, he climbed the steps to her room, knocking and calling out her name. There was no answer.

He knocked again, hesitating, then opened the door. She
was fast asleep. How could anyone sleep so late with the
sun streaming down on her? He stood over her bed, looking.
Her face was pink, crushed against the pink pillow, her body
twisted around in an inverted question mark. She could be
four years old, he thought.

"Louey?" No response. He spoke louder: "Louey?" She
groaned. "You awake?" He touched her shoulder gently.

"Who wants to know?" she muttered, turning over on
her stomach with a loud sigh.

"It's past noon, Louey."

"Think that's funny?" she said into the pillow. After a
moment she pulled the covers around her as if unwilling
to let even the air come between herself and slumber.

He smiled at her furrowed brow; he'd never seen anyone
so ferociously dedicated to sleeping.

"My mother's beginning to wonder if you survived the
night."

She turned over on her back, this time with less of the
sheet following her. To his shock he realized that she was
naked under the blankets, and out of them, too, for much
as he wanted not to believe his eyes, her breasts were exposed
as she flung an arm over her eyes in protest against the
light.

He nearly bent to cover her, stopping as his hands hovered
suspiciously close to her bare flesh. Christ. After all the
trouble he'd taken to undress her the night she'd gotten
drunk and passed out at his place, here she was, displayed
as matter-of-factly as could be. He looked away, then looked

back for an instant. Her skin was so creamy, like a little girl's, but she wasn't a little girl, with beautiful breasts that called out to be cupped, caressed, concealed by his hands. Jesus, enough of this; he bent to tug the blanket over her, but her arm had it pinned too securely to move. He was in the process of trying again when she moved the arm that was shielding her face and surveyed him with two narrow blue smudges. He had never seen anyone so asleep with her eyes open; her face was barely recognizable.

"What are you doing?"

"Covering you up."

She looked down at herself and color rose in her cheeks. "How friendly." She tugged the sheet, then pulled the blanket completely over her head, shaking with laughter. "I'll just be a moment, thanks. Have to get 'em ready to point at your mother."

"That's okay," he said. "You will have some explaining to do about the sheer amount of sleep you've managed to accumulate, though. It's nearly one."

The layers were lowered abruptly. "Why didn't you wake me earlier?"

"We were counting on putting you on the mantel, after we had you stuffed." He sat on the bed next to her and toyed with the pattern on the bedspread.

"Tell you who'll get stuffed," she muttered. He looked at her creased face and laughed.

"Not too cheerful in the mornings, eh?" The pillow she hurled at him only seemed to confirm that he was right.

After he'd seen to her breakfast ("fried eggs, fried bread, fried milk"), Clay ran into town to do some errands for his mother. Everywhere he looked it seemed that people were staring at him; he'd forgotten what it felt like to live in a small town. Was it his imagination, or did things seem shabbier, the people frailer, more subdued?

The last thing he expected on his return was to find Louey and his mother earnestly engaged in conversation. From the distance he could see them sitting together on the patio, the sunlight glinting down on Louey's face, the greenery against his mother's hair a pretty sight, her obligatory tall drink at her side. He nearly stopped in his tracks when he saw his mother's face, more animated than it had been since his father had left. Louey gestured emphatically with her hands. He could only wonder what they might be talking about so heatedly. As he came closer, he noticed another unusual sign—his mother's drink was hardly touched, and the full pitcher next to her seemed to indicate that it was her first. He hastened his approach, making sure they heard him.

"Oh, Clay dear." His mother's face closed instantly, and the two women faced him blankly, as if caught doing something illicit. "Done so soon?"

"I've been gone over two hours. Missed me terribly, I see." He seated himself beside her on the ground and nodded to Louey. "Everything is so damned slow around here; I'd forgotten what it was like."

"You're just out of practice, darling," his mother said. Louey studied him, as if searching for secrets between him and his mother.

"So what have you two been talking about?"

At this his mother took a large sip. He regretted having intruded. How could his own mother be uneasy at the sight of him?

"Your mother and I have been talking about men," Louey said. She cocked her head, waiting for his wisecrack.

"Had a thing or two to teach Mama, I'll bet," he said.

"Louey has been very enlightening." His mother surveyed him almost warmly. To his surprise, she reached out and took his hand. He bent to kiss her soft cheek, warm from the sun. He had loved his mother so much when he was little there were times he was overcome with a feeling of panic at the thought of losing her. "You are a sight for sore eyes, Clayton."

"I should hope so," he remarked. "I got all my mother's looks, after all."

"Now that is the truth," his mother said, patting his cheek. A quiet overtook the three of them suddenly, and for a little while they sat gazing out across the tall grass and gently sloping hills, listening to the birds, content.

"Where do you go to get away?" Louey asked after dinner.

"Have I got something to show you." He wiped his hands with a towel, finished with the dishes. "Come with me."

They walked through a veritable forest of tall brush and uncivilized terrain. How had he maneuvered through this when he was a boy? Clay wondered, gazing at a lone wildflower.

"It's so warm here," Louey mused. "And so quiet."

"You're just used to the screams of drunks and murdered editors."

"True."

Finally they reached his destination, the haven of his childhood. The pond was still and gleaming, as if it had been waiting for him, undisturbed, an oasis quietly nestled in the middle of wild, untamed brush.

"This," she said, "is something."

"I think of it as my own private lake."

She gazed across the water. "Did you come here a lot with friends when you were a little kid?"

"Nope." He thought of his sister, swallowing. "Not really."

"You never brought girls here?" She snorted. "Come on. This is a perfect setup."

"Well . . ." He wondered if he could tell her about Charlene, but couldn't think of a way to put it that wouldn't make him sound like a jerk. "I had a girlfriend, but I never took her here."

"Why?" She sat down at the edge of the pond, smoothing the ground with her feet.

He stood looking out onto the water. "She wasn't someone you could really share things with. She didn't care about much."

"Except you."

He sat down next to her. "Sometimes not even that. She had fun displaying me, and I guess I had fun having as much sex as was humanly possible." He shook his head. "I can't imagine how I kept on with it. I'm so damned— things just take me over, and I let them. I hate myself for it."

She was silent for a moment. "You're not so bad."

They lay back, resting on their elbows and looking out over the shimmering expanse. "So beautiful," he murmured.

"Did you love her?"

"Don't think I've ever been in love." It gave him a queer feeling in the pit of his stomach to say it, as if he were deceiving her. "I used to come here with my sister."

She glanced at him. "You never told me you had a sister before today." He nodded, looking at his feet. "Is she the girl in the picture by your bed?"

He ran his fingers through the dirt. "She killed herself when I was nineteen."

"Oh, Clay." She put a hand on his knee; he felt it even after she had taken it away. "Were you very close?"

"Not close enough to stop her."

"No one can do that." She sighed. "I used to think of killing myself, when I was younger. I felt so"—she frowned— "I don't know, so different when I was a kid. There weren't many Jews where I grew up, for one thing, just these blond cheerleader types." She stopped, sneering. "No offense."

"I never made the squad, myself." He studied her. "Did you have many gay friends?"

"I don't know." She laughed. "I didn't know *I* was gay

until I was nearly in college. I just knew I didn't feel like talking about shopping and makeup."

"Or boys."

"I guess no one feels normal in high school. It's funny; I guess most people wouldn't be gay if they had the choice, but I'd feel so *deprived* if I weren't. I feel so lucky—I can't explain it without sounding ridiculous. It's—it gives everyone you know the chance to be their best selves, in a way. Do you know what I mean?"

"Once you tell them, you mean?"

"Somehow when you're open about something people expect you to be ashamed of, they surprise you by not being nearly as small-minded as you assume they'll be. Most are actually far more sensitive than you've given them credit for."

"Do many people disappoint you?"

She shook her head. "You know, when I told my mother I was gay, she said she wished I was straight, because it would make life easier."

"Easy's overrated."

"I know!" She touched his leg. "I asked her if she'd rather not be Jewish if she'd had the choice, because it would be easier."

"It's no gift being average. At least you have things that make you special."

"I'd hate to be conventional." She smiled. "I told my mother I thought life was fuller when you don't take everything for granted. I'm glad I know what it means to fight for things."

"And to have things to fight for. My life was completely programmed."

"Do you think your sister felt that way?"

He stared at his feet. "She could have been a great musician. She was twenty times more talented than I am." His voice sounded hollow. "She could have used someone to help her appreciate being different."

She touched his arm. "When Kevin died, I started thinking about losing everyone I loved. I'd call my mother just to make sure she was still alive. I think maybe it was the suddenness of it, his just being dead one day without warning; maybe if he'd been sick for a while I wouldn't have felt so panicked." She sat up and took off her shoes, trailing her toes in the water. "I don't understand why I'm so unnerved by this. You'd think having my father die would have prepared me."

"It never goes away completely. And Kevin was just a boy."

"Younger than I am." Her voice faltered.

"You have to give yourself time. You can't live forever in a state of paralysis."

"Not in New York, that's for sure."

"When I first moved, people back here said, Be careful, in New York they kill you on the street just as soon as look at you. If I'd listened to them, I would have spent my days locked up in my apartment. You ride the subway? they'd say, horrified, In the evenings? As if I'd confessed to grand larceny. A person can lock himself in away from life forever if he worries about what might happen. Hell, I could get killed here falling down in my own bathtub."

"It'd take days to find you, too." She swished the water back and forth. "I agree with you, I do. I know I can't live in fear—but I still can't sleep at night. I tell myself I'll always have my memories of Kevin and I should be grateful for the friends I do have, but . . ."

"I wish I could help you."

"You do." She looked over at him almost shyly. "I never expected it to help so much just to talk to you about it. You understand what I feel without looking at me as if I'm having some sort of nervous breakdown." She squeezed his arm, then jumped to her feet, stretching her arms toward the sky as if in supplication. "So is this water forbidden, or what?"

"You mean to swim in?"

She lit up. "Can we go for a swim?"

"Uh—if you want, sure. You like to swim?"

"Like to?" She put her hands on her hips, then suddenly pulled down her jeans in one quick motion. After a moment's hesitation, she pulled her shirt over her head, diving in before he had a chance to blink. By the time he'd made up his mind to join her, she had swum the length of the pond and back. "Freezing!" she called out. In the lake she seemed like a completely different person, making her way through the water with such assurance. He'd never seen her do anything physical before, he realized. Taking off everything but his briefs, he jumped in, swimming out to her. "And here I thought you were the delicate type," he teased.

"Didn't expect me to jump naked into your private lake as soon as I got the chance?" She splashed him, but he ducked. "Well, seen two, seen 'em all."

"Not true," he said, and she pondered his words for an instant before splashing him again. "Race you," he dared.

"Silly boy." In a minute they were speeding across the lake. He was panting by the time he'd beat her, but she'd given him a good race; she might even have won, if he hadn't been so much taller.

"Humiliating," she announced when they reached the shore, shaking her hair.

He let her get dressed first, turning his back and doing a few more strokes. The blood was coursing fiercely through his body; he was incredibly happy, as if he'd been given a glimpse of the life he'd always wanted.

He could just turn and lift her in the air, he thought, just reach out and suspend her high above him. It took nearly all the strength he had just to keep his back to her until she'd finished dressing.

Louey hesitated at the doorway to the living room. The music beckoned, but she felt out of place, uninvited, like a prowler.

Clay sat at the piano, playing Chopin as his mother listened in a high-backed chair, her eyes closed and a peaceful smile on her face. She looked at Louey briefly as Louey sat down on the couch, then nodded toward her son.

What a mass of contradictions Clay was! Watching him in earnest concentration on the music, Louey thought of how she'd taken him for someone aimless, thoughtless, casual as air. Yet here he was, playing gorgeous music so sweetly. It was like discovering a secret part of him. The way he treated his mother—gently, as if she were a priceless vase, a wounded bird—fit in with his playing. Glancing at Dulcie, Louey thought she saw her body fill out with the music. She wondered if Clay's mother had ever shown him the surprisingly resilient self she'd revealed to Louey, the side that wanted more.

Clay played for them for hours, fingers flying, lingering to summon poignant melodies. This was life, thought Louey, listening to beautiful music: pure emotion.

"What did you and my mother find to talk about?" he asked her the next night.

"I've never met a woman who hates men so much."

"Dad."

"Yeah." She thought of the confusion on his mother's face as she'd spoken of her husband. "She hates herself for having loved him."

"But all men aren't like my father. She hasn't taken an interest in anyone else since he left."

"She can't let herself fall for something any man might tell her, since she was so trusting with your father. She has no faith in her judgment; she made such a terrible mistake."

"Poor Mom. I'd hoped she'd get over it and make a new life for herself. Whatever else it was, this house used to be alive. She was a master at big lavish scenes, making people adore her. Now she seems to have lost the stomach for any of it."

"She thinks she's a failure. The one thing she created, her family, turned out to be completely fraudulent."

He was silent. "I'm not fraudulent."

"No, but she's never made her peace with you. She doesn't trust the love she has for you because in some ways you're an extension of your father. She wants to love you but she hates herself for it."

"Wonderful."

"She's terrified that what she feels for you is as misplaced as what she felt for your father."

"I lost touch with her a long time ago." Her words should have upset him, but he felt calm, as if he now understood clearly a truth he'd always suspected. "I've been at a loss to know what she really does think of me."

"She loves you more than anyone in the world, Clay. When I told her she should be proud of having raised such a good person, it was as if I was confirming some dream she'd been afraid to hope for."

"Right." He was surprised at the bitterness in his voice.

"Right," she said emphatically. "It's no small thing to raise a boy who genuinely cares for women. Most men are filled with contempt or fear, as if women were aliens from another planet."

"We're all obsessed with the same things, aren't we? That's no big revelation."

"But it is, to most men. I told your mother it's because of her that you're not fucked up about women. And look at what fabulous women friends you have." She poked his arm.

What a heel he was; now she was congratulating him on his hypocrisy.

"We are friends, aren't we?" she said softly.

He met her eye and nodded. To his surprise, he realized it was true.

"Well . . ." Clay pulled the car up to Louey's apartment.

"I had a wonderful time." She yawned, stretching after the long ride. "Thank you so much, Clay. I feel almost human again."

"What did I tell you?"

"No fooling you." She poked him playfully, and Clay looked down at his hands on the steering wheel, suddenly unwilling to face the abrupt end of their visit. He would never again have such an opportunity to be with her continuously, to have her all to himself, he realized. Watching her sleep part of the way home had been even harder than on the way out.

"It'll be strange not seeing you every day," she said as if reading his mind. The wistfulness in her voice stabbed at him.

"Well, we could . . ."

"How about dinner Friday? What the hell, I could even cook. I think my kitchen still works."

She was probably just being kind to repay his mother's hospitality. "I'd love to."

"We'll see about that after you taste my cooking." She laughed. "Well, toots"—she leaned over and kissed him on the cheek—"can't put off the post-partum blues any longer."

He turned to kiss her, but she had already slid out of the car (damn his reflexes!) and was reaching in the back seat for her bag. "See you about eight?" he said. "I had a swell time."

"Ditto. Don't let the screams of mortal terror keep you awake."

He waited until she'd gone safely inside and then sat for a few moments until he saw the light of her apartment go on. Tempted to stay and watch her, he shook himself and started the car again.

Friday arrived and Clay prepared for dinner, uncharacteristically nervous. He was unable to decide whether to bring wine or flowers, so finally he gave in and bought a bouquet of purple tulips and a bottle of champagne. Nothing in his closet looked remotely right.

When he arrived (twenty minutes early, for which he compensated by walking around the block six or forty times), he discovered that she wasn't ready. She buzzed him in, greeting him at the door sheepishly in a pair of shorts and a shredded T-shirt that made her look slightly plump and lascivious at the same time. He wanted to throw her against the wall and reduce her to the wreck he'd become; instead, he handed her the flowers. She beamed. Tulips were her favorite, she confessed. She pointed him toward her champagne and left to change her clothes.

Just take those off and I'll be fine, he thought, no need to put on a stitch. He fixed himself a drink with hands that had started shaking, then filled her glass to the brim. No telling why he was such a bundle of nerves, as he already knew there was no chance for him here. He'd just spent a full week living with her like a brother, for Christ's sake. His first sip didn't sit well on his stomach, so he put down his glass.

When he looked up she was framed in the doorway,

grinning unabashedly in the dress he'd bought her, holding the tulips in one hand and a tall glass vase in the other.

"They were so beautiful I nearly stapled them to me instead of bothering with the dress. Here, help me arrange them."

He jumped up and took the flowers as she went to get water, wondering if everything was going to take so much effort this evening. Louey seemed a little nervous as well, no doubt unaccustomed to having a formal dinner guest.

"You look just beautiful in that dress."

"Thanks. One of my admirers gave it to me, to try to turn me into a lady."

"How'd it work?"

"Nothing's *that* good." She picked up her drink and winked at him, grinning and depositing herself next to him on the couch. She wore the gown as if it were a sweatshirt and jeans, yet if anything she looked more lovely than if she'd been aware of its effect.

Dinner was a blur; he was conscious of her laughing at jokes he didn't realize he was making and of the glow of her skin in the evening light. Though he'd now spent many nights with her, this evening seemed different, suffused with an odd tension. Was he imagining it?

The meal was a surprise, haphazard but delicious. She confessed that once she had made a dish using all the dried red peppers left over from a friend's effort to cook for her, not realizing how potent they were. Her guests had sat politely through as much of the meal as they could bear, then one by one had bolted to the kitchen for relief.

"Good thing you have other friends to try these things out on first."

She took her glass from the kitchen table, walking across the open room to the couch, and announced that coffee and dessert would be served shortly. He joined her, loosening his tie.

"Clay," she said softly, after a pause. "Are you ever going to start working on the book again?"

He grimaced. "I don't know. It seems so far in the past, so trivial somehow."

"It's not a bit trivial. You're a good writer."

"I'm stalled at the ending; I go blank."

"If it were a book you were reading, how would you want it to end? Maybe if you decided what your real message is, how you feel deep down, something would come to you."

"Love is very different from what I thought it was." He considered. "Not that I know what it *is*."

"I always thought I knew what it was." She traced the rim of her glass. "I had it, after all, with a bang, as it were. But lately I've realized I had better redefine my expectations, because I'll never have that again. And I certainly couldn't bear ever losing it again."

"Life has to go on, you know. What if you had a lover who died? You wouldn't want never to love anyone again, would you?"

"Mia didn't die." He heard tears threatening. "One thing Kevin taught me was that death is the only thing we have no control over. Mia's leaving me wasn't a senseless freak accident; it was something she did, something she did to me. I tried to think of her as dead before, but now I know it's completely different. He didn't abandon me; he was just taken away. I won't ever have the chance to see him again, to hear his sweet little voice." She shrugged as a tear rolled down her cheek. "Mia wasn't taken; she left. She chose to go. And the woman that's out there somewhere, alive, isn't the person I thought I loved, or she could never have stopped loving me, as if I were just a—" Her mouth set. "I shouldn't have expected her to be my fantasy, anyway. No one can live up to that."

When had she come to this conclusion? "So," he said. "What's the solution?"

"Damned if I know. I just figured *this* out, after all."

But I love you, he imagined saying, what about me? He shook himself, tossing down a drink. Why? To ruin the friendship they had? To see a flicker of surprise and disappointment, maybe even disgust, on her face? He had better go home before it came to that. "Well, Louey"—he roused himself—"I'd better go before your night is totally shot."

"You haven't had dessert." She sounded surprised; was she also disappointed?

"You must be tired."

"I wouldn't mind getting out of this dress, I'll tell you that."

He gnashed his teeth; only she could make a comment like that in total innocence, only she would be so blind as to what she was doing to him. "Thanks for a lovely dinner," he managed.

"Really, can't you stay a little longer? It's been such a nice evening."

The unvarnished request in her voice was what finished him. She had no idea. She was pressing him to stay because she liked having him around; she had never given a thought to what raced through his mind every moment he spent with her.

"No, dammit, I can't stay," he said between gritted teeth. She looked at him with such surprise that he found himself glaring; damn her obliviousness! "Don't you know anything at all? Of all people, you should be the first to see the irony here." He tried to lower his voice. "I can't stay another minute or I'll rip that fucking dress off you, don't you understand? And don't think I don't realize how ridiculous I am. I've been in love with you for months and I'll be damned if I can take another minute of it!"

The room was suddenly quiet. He could hear the sound of his voice echoing, his breathing, every painful swallow he took. He was afraid to look at her now; he wanted to laugh, or scream, but all he could do was stand and wait to hear the cold rebuttal in her voice, now that he'd done it.

"Oh," she replied calmly. He looked at her, startled. "Well, I guess you should go, then, if that's how you feel."

He crumbled into a chair, his head in his hands, his shoulders shaking. "Jesus Christ, Louey," he said into his hands. "I swear most of the time I didn't feel this way, I really just liked you."

"Is the fucking dress safe for the moment, or should I go change?"

He looked up, surprised at her dry tone, which she raised an eyebrow to acknowledge. He could feel his face flush under her gaze, but he also felt strangely exhilarated. It was out now, finally, and she didn't seem to hate him.

"So you've been in hell," she said. "You've hidden it pretty well."

"I was ashamed of it. It's not exactly the kind of thing you'd approve of, now is it?"

"I guess I'd have taken it all wrong—gotten insulted or something."

"Are you?"

She looked at her lap, scratching her fingers against the shiny material. "Don't seem to be." His heart leapt. "So what are you going to do about this?"

"Drink myself into a stupor, I guess," he answered, glum again—what havoc his emotions were wreaking with him! "That is, unless you might possibly consider—" His voice faltered.

"What?"

She was going to make him say it. "You—uh, giving it a try, you and me." It lurched out.

"You want me to sleep with you?" She sounded faintly incredulous; what had she thought he was talking about, anyway? Just hearing her say it sent his pulse racing again. Jesus, he was like an adolescent.

"Well," he forged ahead. "I mean, if you think you could care for me at all, you might—we, we might see whether . . ." He looked up and their eyes caught, stuck. He swallowed. "Does it make you—when you think about it, do you feel—does the idea horrify you?" He couldn't look away, though he couldn't bear what he was sure to see on her face.

"I never thought about it," she said.

"Oh." He sagged, deflated. Now he was going to have to get up and go home, somehow manage to say good night to her. "I just think love is rare enough when you do find it, you shouldn't pass up a chance to—to—" He faltered. The strain of the last few hours, being so close, then losing, was more than he could bear. He turned to go, his head heavy on his shoulders. "Look, your friendship has always been very important to me, and—"

"Clay."

He stole a glance at her. She was taking off her shoes calmly, gazing at him. Then she put her hands in her lap and looked down at them, her face flushed and bashful, as if she were a little girl. He scarcely knew what to think. When he realized that she was trembling, a wave of heat overtook him; was she actually considering it? He was unable to take his eyes off her. She lifted her gaze to his finally, the unspoken question making his heart pound so fiercely he could hardly breathe. They stared at each other for what seemed like hours; then he heard her swallow. As if it were an activity he'd just learned, he rose and sat beside her, putting a hand on her shoulder.

She closed her eyes, making his pulse race. "Don't expect too much," she said in a low voice.

When Clay traced the curve of her bare shoulders with his lips, Louey began to shake so convulsively he could hear her teeth rattle in her head. "Jesus," she muttered under her breath, shifting on the couch so that her back looked even more stiffly upright than it had before. When Clay went to kiss her, she turned her head instinctively, so that he found himself sampling her neck instead; when he cupped one of her breasts, she started from him as if burned. "Please don't do that." She spoke in the most wretched voice he had ever heard.

Clay's skin went cold. Removing his hand and lips from her as one might retreat from a child whose parent had discovered her in the process of being molested, he studied her in bewilderment. She would not meet his eyes but sat, downcast and miserable.

"I'm sorry," she managed.

He said nothing, hardly knowing what response would be appropriate. "So am I" would sound more like accusation than self-indictment.

"I thought—"

"You thought you could go through with it, and you can't." As if he were some punishment she had to suffer— and for what crime?

"I don't know why I just—" The phone interrupted her, and she stared as if she couldn't possibly imagine who could be hounding her. On the third ring she sprang to get it; after her "Hello?" she shifted from one foot to another nervously. "No, it's—how have you been? Me? I'm just—" He watched her stiffen suddenly. "He's—oh." She seemed to deflate before his eyes. "You don't—didn't anybody tell you—?" she went on in even more piteous tones than those which had rebuffed him. He studied the pattern on her sheets, resisting an impulse to sink back, close his eyes, and will himself a happier conclusion to the evening. "He died," he heard her say. "No, in his car. It was an accident. Look, can I—? No, but—" She listened for a long time, turning so her face was totally obscured from him. Finally she broke in. "I'm sorry—can I call you back tomorrow?" Abruptly she hung up, but stayed suspended by the phone as if engaged in conversation. He heard a long sigh; still she didn't turn to face him. After a moment he realized she was crying. Unable to help himself, he went to her, rounding her shoulders with his palms. She turned blindly, burying her face in his chest, and his arms came around her. The warmth of her damp, miserable body as she sobbed against him coursed through him like joy. How could her suffering fill him with both pain and happiness?

She lifted a blotched face to his at last. "An old author of mine," she said, hiccuping twice. "He said it's been too long since he and Kevin and I had a night out on the town." He tightened his arms around her, astonished at the rage that filled him at the cruelty of the coincidence. "Isn't that the dumbest thing you ever heard?"

He nodded, afraid to risk speech, and she began to sob again, until he was drenched and aching. He tried to soothe her, smoothing circles on her heaving back.

"I'm sorry . . . put you through . . . of all the times to . . ." she gulped, lifting her tear-stained face from his chest once more. Before he knew what he was doing, he was kissing her trembling mouth, her hot cheeks, kissing the tears from her eyes, he couldn't stop kissing her and she was kissing him back as if all the need she had was tumbling out of her, kissing him as if possessed. If he had been able to speak, he would have explained that he hadn't meant to kiss her, hadn't planned—but it was impossible to stop, he was out of control, he would happily die if only he would never have to stop just kissing her. By the time he realized he was on the verge of flinging himself on her, she had broken from his arms and fled her own apartment. He stood, shaken, wondering what he was expected to do now.

One week after Clay had decided he'd be happy if he never heard the name Louey again, he came home to find her seated on the stoop of his apartment. She seemed bewildered to find herself sitting there waiting for him. "What," she blurted. "You've got nothing better to do than lie around pining for me?" He wasn't sure just how he felt about this turn of events. "Was it something I said?" she muttered, trying not to look too encouraging.

Inside, she pressed her face to his chest and slipped her hands inside his shirt.

They were like two people who had never even met or spoken. She was unaccountably relieved when he stopped her and asked, "Do you mind if we just lie down for a while?" They were both still fully dressed. "It doesn't make sense for us to be this tense."

"Okay." Her voice sounded unfamiliar. It was different from Mia—different from women altogether. She tried unsuccessfully to stifle a snort of nervous laughter. Soon she was giggling hysterically. "Everything you'd dreamed it would be, huh?"

"Well . . ."

"Aaaah," she caved in, weak from laughter, flouncing onto his bed.

"Are you wearing anything under that?" he asked, collapsing next to her. She was buttoned up from top to bottom.

"What do *you* think?"

"You might be more comfortable in one of my sweatshirts." He watched her features soften, threatening to collapse again.

"Ever the gentleman." She rose, walking over to his closet. "Close your eyes." She sounded annoyed.

"Fine time to be modest."

"It's finally dawning on me the danger I'm in." He could hear the sound of clothing rustling, off, then on. She cleared her throat and he opened his eyes to see her coming toward him in a long shirt.

"Do you feel in danger?" he asked.

"If you must know—" She paused, gingerly leaning her body against his. His pulse raced. "It's not that I'm scared of you—" She stopped. "Well—" Again her body was trembling under his hands, even as he tightened his hold.

"Louey?" He couldn't help running his fingers over the curve of a shoulder; the flesh on her arm rose as if from a chill. "We don't have to do anything, you know."

"I like you," she said; now her teeth were chattering, and she laughed, embarrassed. "Funny, it never was this much trouble before. You'd think I was a virgin."

His heart sank; somehow she had the knack of reminding him all too clearly what it was he was actually doing. He loosened his hold on her, sighing. "Louey—" She sneezed. In his mind's eye he was already leaping out of bed and getting her clothes when she reached out to trace the path of his downturned mouth.

"Soft," she said to herself. With this she did something that halted his breathing: kissed him once, twice, three times softly on the lips. His body seemed unbearably hot; she parted his lips and dipped into his mouth, retreated, dipped again. He groaned, crushing her to him. She kept kissing him, brushing his lips endlessly, her hands stealing over him, then darting away as if surprised by what they found.

It was unbelievable. He had never felt this way from only kissing. He was afraid he would come just from the feel of her lying across him, her weight on his body and her mouth lowering itself onto his as if they'd never come up for air.

"Wait, wait—" he whispered, frantic to stop her before he lost all control—how could anyone kiss like that?—and she sat up, frightened, her face flushed.

"What's wrong?"

"Nothing, only—only—" He caught his breath, confessing, "It's too much."

"That's supposed to be my line."

"Well, but wasn't it—for you?"

In answer she kissed him, kisses that seemed to go directly to his core, his body screaming as if he'd never had sex before.

"Clay?"

He opened his eyes, unaware he'd shut them, hardly knowing where to look. This was much worse than he'd anticipated. He'd thought getting her to sleep with him, sleeping with her, would get her out of his system, calm him down once and for all. Yet this was a catastrophe in the making, clearly, if a few minutes of kissing could bring him to this point.

"Clay?" She touched his shoulder. "Could I ask a favor?"

"If—sure."

"Do you think you could take off every stitch of clothing you have on?" She grinned, wicked. "Nothing personal. It's just I've never seen a man naked before."

Now he was bright red, but he rose and complied, though he hardly knew what to do with his hands when he was done.

"Hmm." She studied him.

He hadn't been this shy since he was a teenager. "Doesn't seem exactly fair," he muttered.

"Don't get all hot and bothered." She tried unsuccessfully to stifle another giggle.

"Am I amusing you?"

"No," she answered gently, rising to stand before him. She trailed a hand so lightly across his chest it made him shiver. With an effort he kept his hands at his sides, but she inspected him freely, surprised at his intake of breath as she caressed him.

"Sensitive," she mused. She could understand, suddenly, why gay men liked men's bodies; his was lovely, nearly as graceful as a woman's.

"Yeah," he managed.

She drew closer, still not relinquishing her hold on him. "What does it feel like to put it inside someone?"

Jesus! She was serious. He hardly knew what to answer her. "Incredible."

"Must be." She pushed his cock against the shielded front of her and he groaned softly. "Hmm." She rubbed him up and down the fabric. He closed his eyes, feeling all the energy in his body concentrated on the small part of him barely touching her.

"Louey," he said, stopping her hands at last, "you're driving me crazy." He unbuttoned the shirt, pulling the fabric away from her body, and she flushed as he bared her breasts. Then his hands were acting of their own accord, stroking her skin, cupping her breasts as if it were his right to touch her this way, as if she wouldn't mind his doing it.

"Am I?" she asked, kissing him so hungrily his whole body responded. He could feel her heart pounding against his, her breasts crushed against his chest, as she kissed him again and again. He bruised her lips, her neck, the swell of her breasts. He was disheveled, out of control, swept away by something he didn't understand.

What on earth is happening to me? Louey thought as waves of heat swept across her body. This wasn't like her, not like her at all.

"What are you doing?"

The blood was rushing to her face.

"You'll burn if you don't put some of this on. Your skin isn't used to California sun." Mia continued to rub lotion into Louey's lower back, pulling down the pants of her bathing suit and cooling her exposed skin with the moisture. "Lift up," Mia said. Her voice was completely cool, matter-of-fact. I'm making too big a deal of this, Louey told herself; the rest of the world wasn't as painfully modest as she was. She lifted her body so Mia could pull the bottom off completely. Mia continued rubbing the cream into her, using both hands. Louey tried to make herself feel drowsy, lulled by Mia's rhythmic hands, but her nerves seemed to be on edge. Mia reached up to unhook the top of Louey's suit, pulling it away from the sides of her body, rubbing some of the oil into the line on her back.

"Turn over."

"What?"

The breeze played along the back of Louey's legs and neck. Neither of them spoke for a moment. Louey nearly lost track of where she was, hearing Mia's sentence shatter into the distance. Then her voice broke through again, clear and insistent.

"Turn over, Louisa."

She obeyed, trying to be as nonchalant as Mia, hoping Mia would mistake her blush for a flush from the heat. She couldn't stop her sharp intake of breath as Mia's fingers came down on her breasts, rubbing cream into them gently, and Louey turned her head to one side, trying to harden herself against the effect Mia's hands were having on her. If Mia realized what Louey was feeling, she'd be lost, Mia would be horrified, her family would—oh! Mia's hands cupped each of Louey's breasts, resting, heavy, and she was filled with a dull pain that was almost unendurable. What was wrong with her?

"Mia," she ventured, about to ask if Mia would mind if they didn't put any more lotion on her, but before she could speak, Mia had bent her head to her and was rubbing her mouth where her hands had been. Louey let out a sob. Mia had her tongue on Louey's nipples, teasing and swirling as she brushed her open lips across them, going from one breast to another, nipping and sucking. Surely she couldn't be doing this, and in public—her hands trailed down to Louey's thighs as her mouth continued its onslaught, her fingers searching Louey out, drifting to the exact center of her pain—God! Her mouth found its way to Louey's, and soon there was nothing at all Louey could do to stop her.

Louey woke to find not Mia but Clay making love to her. Her body felt unfamiliar, disoriented; how had this strange man gotten in her bed?—but this wasn't her bed at all. Everything he did set off some alien, unexpected heat in her, as if there were some chemical bond between them that neither had suspected. It was so unlikely a boy should provoke such feelings in her that she wanted to laugh; it was silly, false, out of the question. She would have stopped him and explained that this was nothing she cared to be doing—if only she could get her body to agree.

If anyone had said to Clay a year ago that he would find himself one sunny summer afternoon preparing to walk down Fifth Avenue surrounded by gay people in the tens of thousands, he would probably have answered, "You should watch those pharmaceuticals." Yet here he was.

The decision now at hand was whether they should march with gays from Yale or (as Louey was inclined to favor) Gays for Grains. Clay himself would not have minded marching with the Gays for Pot, who not only got to ride the biggest truck in the parade (festooned with six-foot marijuana leaves and an enormous joint) but also had the choice of wearing lovely bandanas to obscure their faces if they wished. (These guys can't be gay, Clay thought: with their long, bedraggled hair, scruffy tie-dyed clothes and sixties druggie music?)

They stood with several friends of Louey's at the corner of the park and Fifty-ninth Street, watching the Gay Pride Parade march past them. Clay was astonished at the sheer volume of people out on a Sunday, waiting to cheer, or stare. This went on every year and he had never even known that it existed? It boggled his mind, like the underground gay world and every detail Louey knew by heart—sex clubs that wouldn't admit men if they wore cologne ("too sissy"), what the rainbow-colored handkerchiefs once had meant ("those days are gone").

"What do you say to spending the Lord's Day together, babyface?" he'd asked her earlier that week, and Louey had been forced to tell him she was going to the march. After a pause, she had invited him (somewhat reluctantly, it seemed to Clay) to come along.

She'd seemed so certain that he would refuse he'd been compelled to prove her wrong. "Sure," he said, "I'll wear that special outfit you got me . . ."

It was not at all what he'd expected. Crowds of people beamed at him—so many pretty women holding hands; huge, burly men; flamboyant black drag queens. "Look at those guys"—Louey pointed as a group of someone's grandparents marched by. Clay stared; how could they be gay? "I love it," Louey added. (Of course gay people grew old, Clay chided himself, just like anyone.) One pair of men carried a sign that said "52 years together," which outdid everyone he knew. There were even gay cops, though their friends on duty gave them a wide berth, with no sign of emotion on their faces.

The college contingents made Clay feel old, an unfamiliar—and unpleasant—sensation. The biggest college groups were Yale and Harvard. "Don't you think Yale calls to us?" teased Louey. "Rally those pretensions and we'll join 'em." The next float held a sign up: Gays for Grains. She grabbed his arm—"We have to"—tugging him.

"Don't you think your loud, persistent ridicule will start to get to them?"

"You're such a *nice* boy." She sneered, giving in. A Gay Daddy passed them, waving.

Clay glanced at her as a collection of people with AIDS approached. If Louey were worried that her other friends might die, she hadn't shared her fears with him. A mass of

Catholics followed, and then, fittingly, a group in leather. "Sick," said Annie, one of Louey's friends.

"People think *we're* sick," Louey pointed out.

"Everyone has fantasies. They just shouldn't act them out."

"Where have I heard that argument before? You don't think people say the same thing about you and Joyce? Christ, those guys aren't hurting anyone."

"Just each other," Clay said.

"I'm not saying I understand it," Louey replied, "but everyone defines things differently. We can't all be stock-brokers in three-piece suits—now there's a scary image. You know, one man's meat . . ."

". . .'s another boy's linguini?" offered Clay.

"You're too kinky for me." Annie glanced at Clay to make her point.

"That's me," Louey sighed. "Miss Perversion. If my mother only knew."

"I thought you tell your mother everything."

Clay thought of the one time he'd answered Louey's phone when she'd been in the shower; Meredith Mercer had seemed baffled by the fact of him. What did Louey tell her family, he thought, if her mother didn't even know he existed? Any day now, she was sure to take him by the arm and say, "Like you madly, let's be friends."

"I never thought I would be doing this," she'd told him after they'd made love the first time. She seemed as undone by the sex as he was, yet any time he tried to find out how she felt, she called him her "sex buddy" as if warning against taking it too seriously.

"So what do you think, my little petunia?" she asked now, turning to him. "Are we having fun yet?"

"Yeah," he admitted, surprised.

"Everything a boy could hope for?"

"And then some."

"Do you mind marching?"

He didn't know how he felt about thousands of people staring at him, but he wasn't going to admit that. "I don't know about everyone staring at me, though."

"They'll be eating their hearts out, moose lips."

He smiled. "The sacrifices I make for principle."

He'd never seen her so energetic—or so elated. As she flirted with old friends and strangers (an inordinate number of strange gay men treated her as if she were their oldest pal, which didn't make sense), he realized she was in her element. He felt a twinge. Why was this more important to her than the way they felt together? He could share the spirit of the crowd: so joyous, even brave. Yet why couldn't she be equally elated being with him?

"Having fun?" Louey called out as a cop rolled his eyes at a drag queen on roller skates. The officer met Louey with a blank expression that might as well have been a sneer. "Asshole," she muttered to Clay. "I can't believe how unfriendly these cops are."

"This is work for them," Clay said.

"It takes a twisted spirit not to have a good time in this crowd."

"They're just eating their hearts out, moose lips." When she turned to him and beamed, he prayed: Just give me this, this one thing. I can make you happy, he thought, smiling back at her. If only she would let him.

Louey dreamt that she was being lavished with heated attention. Mia? she thought for a moment, reaching out to empty bedclothes before recognition and awareness dawned on her. Why did she continue to feel Mia's presence so vividly after all this time? It must be all this business with Clay unsettling her.

It had been several months since they'd started—well, she didn't know what to call it. Since their friendship had grown sexual. She hadn't actually slept with him the way he wanted; for some reason, she didn't seem to be able to get herself to do that, she didn't know why. He'd been surprised and frustrated at first, she could see, and irritated with himself for not having thought to bring contraceptives, as if that was what was holding her back. She didn't understand what the big deal was; wasn't it enough to be completely naked and make each other incredibly excited until they came? Did they have to fuck?

It seemed so odd to be involved with a man, so completely out of character. She would walk down the street on weekends and be struck with the unlikeliness of it; how her family would react if they knew! Sometimes she had to laugh at the notion that suddenly she was a conventional woman.

She couldn't believe she had so much passion for Clay, she who couldn't think of men's bodies without going blank. Yet when she touched Clay, it was as if some current flowed between them, as if they had secret lives outside their clothed ones.

Clay would run into her on the street and light up, throw both his arms around her, kiss her, stroke her shoulders in the open air. Even more unsettling than how instantly and fiercely she became aroused was the fact that no one seemed to notice. So this was what it was like to be straight. Clay had no idea how lucky he was to be able to express what he felt without giving it a second thought; he could nibble on her earlobe as they stood in line at the movies, he could walk up to her on the street and pull her to him, nuzzling her hair, his arms around her middle, cradling her from behind. When she and Mia had sat together on the subway talking closely but not touching, people had glared at them, though she'd thought she had been imagining their disapproval. In contrast, everyone seemed to give her being with Clay their blessing. She could publicly molest Clay, *anything*, and no one else would even notice, much less raise an eyebrow. If it hadn't been so educational, it would have made her angry. She'd thought she'd been free with Mia, heedless of the world's opinion, but she saw now that she'd held herself back without even realizing it. From now on, she would never be able to accept anything less.

How she felt about being with him was another matter. She had never been so lavished with affection, it was true. Still, she couldn't believe he never tired of being with her; sometimes when she could quite happily have been alone, when she would almost have preferred to be alone, she couldn't understand why he didn't feel as she did. She certainly did not approve of being so compatible with a boy. It seemed a mockery of everything she was, a dirty joke; it made a sham of how she felt about the world. Still, it wasn't

Clay's fault. He was as easygoing as ever, without lurking expectations of a sudden transformation on her part, as far as she could tell. My mother would be so *confused*, she thought.

It had been odd, the first few weeks, not really wanting him to call, afraid to lead him on. If only he were female, she wouldn't find herself remembering how it felt to hold a woman's body, longing for some woman, any woman, to make love to. She couldn't bear to be without the way she'd felt walking down the street with Mia: never again to see that flash of a reciprocal smile on a stranger's face at the most unexpected moments. Yet when she saw Clay, her doubts receded; she was happy, too, if in a different way. She had no clue: what should she make of it, this thing they had? What kind of future could it hold?

She cared for him. Denying that because it didn't make sense to her would be like denying her love for Mia because it didn't make sense to most of the world. How could he have wanted her so much without betraying any hint of how he'd felt? She shook her head. The situation was too perverse to comprehend.

Clay looked up from a bench in Riverside Park to see her striding toward him. His heart leapt. Why was it that each time he saw her unexpectedly he was filled with such elation it neared pain? Perhaps the strangest part of it was how intense his physical response to her was; denied a conventional outlet, he was constantly aroused, as if their time together were all foreplay. Simply picking up her hand and playing with her fingers got him hard. When he held her in his arms each time she told a snide, self-mocking story, every particle of her body would seem to touch each particle of his, suffusing him with sensation. He was almost scared to fuck her, lest it disillusion her—hell, disillusion both of them. How could sex be any better than it was already?

They were both completely out of hand. No doubt she'd been prepared for something brutish—or, at best, perfunctory, but this was almost frighteningly intense, surpassing anything he'd thought sex could be. He'd never been attuned to any woman's body as he was to hers. He'd been amazed, when he tried to imagine what she felt and what she wanted, how his own body responded.

One day they were sitting watching an old movie on television when she began idly playing him, looking straight ahead, engrossed in the movie as she stroked his arm lightly up and down, then moved to stroke his leg as lightly, up and down, then landed softly between his legs, pressing him until they were both breathing heavily. When he tried to move, she held him back; the same for reaching out to her or loosening his clothes. In a way, discomfort heightened his excitement; she manipulated him carelessly, almost rudely, through the cloth, grasping him so that he groaned. She mauled his chest through the fabric—none of her touched skin—and finally he couldn't take any more but pushed her down, flinging himself on her. She turned her head, refusing to kiss him, and he followed the defiant mouth, unable to get any satisfaction. What was she doing? "Louey?"

"Get off me," she said.

Numbed by her tone, he sat on the floor against the couch, waiting for an explanation. His body ached for release, but he couldn't move until she told him why she was acting so strangely.

She let the movie continue playing and rose, standing in front of him and slowly taking off her clothes, holding his eyes. Despite himself, his own body prickled in response, as if hypnotized by her mood. She let her pants drop to the floor, stepping out of them and kicking them aside, hooking her fingers into silken underpants, starting to slide them down off her. Her eyes seemed to bore into him as she changed her mind, pulling them back up and standing upright.

Now it was his turn, and he began to slip the shirt over his head, but her eyes cautioned him not to move. She came over to him and removed his shoes and socks; her hands caressing his feet seemed deliciously powerful, as if she could command his body to respond merely by touching him anywhere. She tugged his jeans off with no help from him, pulling his briefs off in the same motion. He was so hard he was nearly past the point of pleasure. She left his shirt on and inched in toward him, brushing her breasts against the front of his shirt, teasing him with them, then nipping at him through the shirt. He was losing his will to resist. She remained silent. Then she sat on him, bringing him tantalizingly near her core despite the strictures of the thin cloth. Only now would she kiss him, moving back each time he tried to respond as if to warn him against daring to enter her mouth. The friction everywhere was agonizing; he was nearly out of his head.

Abruptly she grew still. She seemed very subdued, locked in by the confines of his body, and he opened his eyes, puzzled. "Louey?" he whispered against her neck, and she sighed heavily. "What's the matter?"

"Not one thing," she said against his chest; then she withdrew, walking to the bedroom. He joined her, taking off his shirt along the way. She threw the covers aside and lay down, and he sat beside her, stroking her cheek. She glanced at him, then helped him pull the panties off her.

"So," she began. He lay down beside her, running his hand over her breasts and stomach, propping himself on one elbow to regard her. "Guess who got her period?"

"Someone in this room?"

"Which means we can do it," she said.

"What?" He laid his hand flat on her belly. Her skin was burning. "It's not as if it'll be a first for either of us."

"Clay."

"*Tell* me," he said, exasperated.

"How about it?" She rose to nibble an earlobe, imprinting a trail of heat down his neck. "Wanna try that special thing we've heard so much about?"

He realized he was staring. "Are you sure you want to take the chance?"

"What, now you don't want to?"

"Are you kidding?" He lowered his voice. "I just don't want you to feel . . ."

"Enough stalling, baby, time to reach nirvana." She lay back, then sat up again. "Or should I get on top?"

"Uh—either way." He couldn't believe they were clinically discussing this. "It's easier if you open your legs, though."

"Picky, picky, picky." She looked down at herself, laughing. "Well, fire away."

"Jesus, Louey, you're about as romantic as—lunch meat."

"Sorry." She smiled and lay across him, humming a romantic melody indulgently and then kissing him as she had the very first time: soft, quick kisses that reassured him and made him want more. He trailed his tongue along her neck and slid his fingers down until she moaned into his ear. Years of training made this feel foolhardy, but he was damned if he was going to be the one to be cautious.

"Hmm," she said as they began: odd that it should feel like white noise, painful without really hurting. What a lady, she thought, hearing herself grunt. How did people do this?

"Be sure," he said between gasps, "and tell me," through gritted teeth, "if I'm hurting you." She relaxed her body against his, stroking his back. At first she could only feel him in her but nothing on the rest of her body; then he shifted, broadening his strokes, and her mind went blank with desire.

"Oh," they breathed together as he ground the front of

her and she moved against him, hotter and hotter. Finally they fell, crying out, one after the other. He stayed inside her, his heart pounding against hers.

"God." He spoke at last, rolling off her and resting a dead arm on her stomach. He could still feel the touch of her palms flat on his back.

After a while, she turned to look at him. "So. That's it?" When he turned to her, she broke down, grinning. "All that talk about something so—whimsical."

"Are you all right?"

She pointed to his still-heaving stomach. "Better than you, sugar."

"Give me a minute." He went to embrace her, but before he'd managed to succeed, she'd draped herself across him. "This time I get to be on top," she said. He opened his mouth to protest that he wasn't quite ready for next time, but before he could speak he discovered it was no longer true.

After the fifth month, Louey realized she was doing with Clay what she had never done with Mia: pretending not to be involved with him. The prospect of telling her friends she was sleeping with a man—a *white* man—held so little appeal she couldn't conceive of doing it. "Uh, by the way, girls, guess what I've been up to . . ." Opportunities to slip the news innocuously into conversation were hardly plentiful.

At the office, her assistant handed her messages from Clay with a blank expression on her face; her co-workers seemed far too casual whenever she brought up his name. Suddenly she could understand why bisexuals had such a hard time of it; it was as if she were lying to *everyone*. The straight people she met with Clay simply assumed she was straight, while her gay friends didn't even consider the possibility that she could feel anything but what they did. (Not that she could even consider herself bisexual; she had hardly started leering at pubescent boys on the subway.) What she felt with Clay was some sort of fluke. Jesus, baby, you're disgraceful, she thought, at a loss.

The first mistake Clay made was to suggest celebrating their six-month anniversary. Shock colored Louey's face. "You mean it's been half a year already?"

Oh, I see, he thought; he was some brief aberration in her life, that was how she justified continuing with him.

Their next mistake was going dancing. She seemed uneasy in his arms, looking at the other couples as if incredulous to find herself among so many women out with men. Worse, dancing always reduced him to a raw mass of desire, and she was clearly feeling far from amorous. His worst mistake was stopping her from saying what was bothering her, lest she tell him six months was his deadline; instead, he ordered more and more champagne, staving off despair. He wouldn't let her go. He wouldn't. So what if he wasn't goddamned Mia, so what if she went back to women, as long as she still wanted him.

"Clay—" she started, as the music changed.

"I know," he said. "Let's leave, then."

She opened her mouth, then decided better of it and turned from the dance floor.

After they'd walked several blocks outside, she began again. "Clay, I need to talk to you."

"Let me guess." A sinking feeling filled him. "You think we should spend—"

"Louey?" They both looked into the face of a tall woman with a gleaming full head of red hair. "Is that really you?"

"Teddy?!" Louey hugged the other woman. "I haven't seen you in a million years!"

"Don't I know it." The other woman looked her up and down, delighted. "You look wonderful. Where the hell have you been? Everyone's been wondering if you've suddenly become too good for the rest of us."

"Too tasteful, certainly," Louey said. She glanced over at Clay and then back at the woman. "This is my friend

Clayton Lee. Clay, meet Theodora Wilkin, the sickest woman in New York."

"And here I thought you held that title." Clay shook the woman's hand.

"Ah, a man who understands." Teddy smiled at him, returning his handshake warmly. She didn't seem at all put off by his presence. (Hell, he realized, she probably thought he was gay.) It was remarkable that they'd never accidentally run into any of her friends before: only a matter of time, he thought, before Mia showed her ugly face again. "Listen," Teddy went on. "You've got to come with me right now. I'm just on my way to a party at Tony's, and if I tell him I let you get away he'll skin me alive."

"Oh, I don't think . . ." Louey turned to Clay, trying to conceal her eagerness. "Clay and I were on our way to—"

"We can't disappoint Tony," Clay said, "now, can we?" The gratitude on her face pained him. "Unless he wouldn't approve of my crashing the party."

"Are you kidding?" Teddy came between them, taking an arm from each and leading them down the street. "Darling, he'll love *you*." Clay caught Louey's eye, and she couldn't help laughing. Teddy joined in, innocently.

The party was everything he feared: beautiful women dancing with each other and pretty men looking to dance with him. So far Louey had resisted dancing with anyone, but he couldn't help noticing the squeals of delight that greeted her with each newly discovered long-lost friend. As each of them embraced her, he felt a pang. Why hadn't they done more together with her friends? She must have feared he wouldn't fit in, or would shame her. He watched her greet the host, a slim black man—and the dancer who had told him Mia's name. Clay felt a twinge: no doubt about it, Mia had to show. Yet Louey clearly wasn't worried. Why was he?

They were really nice here, he thought with surprise some

hours later. They accepted him at once and teased him fondly, as if he were family, home at last. He *was* at home, somehow. So why did he feel so hopeless?

It was the sight of Clay dancing with Tony's ex-boyfriend that did it for Louey. She'd been amazed to see him so at ease with her friends; the average straight man would have been possessive, threatened. Mark took his hand and tried to dip him, and he winked at her, giving Mark his hand back apologetically. He really was wonderful, she thought. She approached him just as the dance was ending and asked to cut in. (Clay, ever the Southern gentleman, was thanking Mark.)

"Disgusting," Tony murmured at the sight of Louey nibbling on Clay's neck; then he gave Clay a wink. "I only wish I could get her to do that to me," he added.

"You'd run shrieking from the room if I ever tried," said Louey.

"You'll never know now, will you?" Tony flounced off in mock offense.

Clay closed his eyes, feeling dreamily contented, as if time were suspended. After the next song, a woman asked each of them to dance. In a little while they left, reassuring their host they'd do their best to fight this perverted business that had gotten hold of them.

This time the silence as they walked to Clay's apartment was comforting instead of tense. When Louey smiled at him, he felt so happy he wanted to crow. Somehow the evening had changed so completely he scarcely believed it. How could a party with her gay friends have made her happier to be with him?

As they neared his place she pulled him to her, backing him against a wall and kissing him, all hot and liquid. He put his hands all over her.

"Wait, wait, we're almost home," she said, laughing.

"What's wrong with here and now?" *She'd* started it.

"Nothing," she said, "but it could be so much more tawdry inside."

When they got home he pulled her to him, and she slid over him deliberately, making him groan. Lowering her breasts against his, she fastened her mouth for a fresh assault, stripping, and he ripped his shirt off, grinding her into him and inhaling her neck, drenching her. He slid down to her bare breasts and she twisted to escape, ticklish, but he forced her into his tongue, his hands firm on her bare back. Her breasts pointed at him as she arched into his mouth. He eased his knee between her legs and she fumbled for him, until he had to take his mouth away from her and strip off the rest of his clothing.

It was only later that Clay wondered if the presence of all those women had been what had excited Louey, and nothing to do with him at all. It was not a thought he liked having.

"Come here often?"

Louey was walking with two packagers and an agent when Mia appeared from out of nowhere and clapped her on the back, smiling down at her.

It was worse than on the subway. This time Mia seemed to want to talk, as if nothing could be as pleasant as a chat with an old pal. Louey froze as two of her friends stopped debating where to go for dinner and examined Mia's beauty; the third stared up Columbus cynically and said rude things to passersby. For the first time Louey wished that Mia were indifferent, elsewhere, gone, but Mia stood and blocked her way, still smiling. At last her grin changed to bewilderment, then shock, when she saw Louey wasn't going to meet her eyes. After what seemed like hours, she dropped her hand from Louey's shoulder and disappeared.

Instantly Louey's friends reinstigated forward motion, putting Columbus Avenue once more under assault. Not mentioning the incident, the three discussed the usefulness of leather, pointing out examples from the streets before them. (No one complained when Louey's contribution proved minimal.)

The years with Mia had been a rich feast. Louey's life hereafter was to be a sip of tea, she saw now, a biscuit eaten hastily over the sink: at best a subtle consommé that would never leave her filled, though it did make her feel noble.

To celebrate the signing of their book contract, the group went (after prolonged drinking) to a dance club. "So, Louey," one packager inquired as they braved a medley of Diana Ross. "Who was that hunk of woman?"

"What woman?" Louey answered. Diana called to her.

"We would all be most displeased to learn that you've been holding out," her friend went on. "We all thought you never went in for that sort of thing. So messy, love, so—cheap. It's going to be a shock when everyone finds out you've got a heart."

"Not anymore," said Louey. Diana grew fainter, and the beginning rumblings of Madonna threatened to erupt into volcanic squeaks. She closed her eyes. "That was my past."

"You gave *that* up?"

"No." Louey lost the will to rumba. "It gave *me* up." The faces around her looked away out of respect for a tragedy even they couldn't comprehend.

Surely in time the lure and memory of Mia would have to fade into oblivion, Louey told herself. For now, all she could do was wait.

"So when are you guys going to move in together full-time?"

Louey brought the salad bowl from the kitchen and handed a glass of wine to her oldest brother, Paul. Her other brother, Danny, was remaining tactfully silent on the whole topic, she noted, and Clay, too, seemed to be keeping a low profile.

"I'm serious," Paul went on. "It's time you made a commitment, Louey. You've been avoiding adulthood long enough."

"Have we met?" (I have so much work to do, thought Louey, I don't have time for this.) She had two novels to edit before the end of the month, exactly two weeks. One week per novel, she groaned: perfect.

"Meal looks great." Danny changed the subject. "Are you sure you cooked this?"

"Clay cooked most of it," Louey said. "I made dessert, though."

A rare family reunion over the coming three-day holiday had brought both of Louey's brothers concurrently through New York, and after an intense campaign to persuade her, Louey halfheartedly agreed to join them in D.C. "I can't," she'd moaned, but Clay told her it would do her good to get away from work—and him. Something in her resisted leaving New York, as if outside the city she would be diluted, forced to live a fraudulent existence.

Louey drank her wine and listened to the lively talk, marveling at the contrast Clay made with her brothers. It should comfort her to have them so clearly approving of him, Clay so obviously genuine in his enjoyment of them, yet she found herself watching, listening as if from a remove. If she were to tell Danny that she was dreaming of Mia again, even felt the stray pang for Mia to have it in her to woo Louey back properly, he would be aghast. Yet the scene in front of her was strangely surreal, like someone else's family. Her brothers welcoming a lover of hers so readily into the family—a rich blond Gentile who didn't even work for a living? It couldn't be.

She was piling dishes in the sink when Clay came up behind her. "Overdose of family?" he whispered, wrapping his arms around her. As he nibbled on an earlobe, she wriggled from him.

"I'm just tired." She wanted to tell him what was bothering her—if only she could figure out what it was.

"Louey!" The sight of her mother's glowing face erased whatever fatigue had accumulated from the journey from New York. It had been nearly a year and a half since Louey had seen her mother, an unusual lapse in what her friends had always considered excessively frequent maternal contact. They embraced; her mother kissed her warmly.

"How's work?"

"Wonderful," she said, not mentioning that every time the phone rang in her mother's house, she would probably have to stop herself from answering it, certain it was an author with a vital problem that couldn't be solved unless she flew back instantly. "I shouldn't be here now."

"Your employer doesn't believe in the sanctity of Martin Luther King Day?"

She smiled. "How could I work for one that didn't?"

"So what's this Paul tells me about your having a boy-friend?" Meredith asked when they had spent some time alone in Louey's old room, going through her closet to throw out old clothes.

"Great," Louey muttered.

"You didn't want me to know?"

"Nothing to know, Mother. I haven't changed." She cradled an old shirt, now sadly outgrown. "Anyway, he's not Jewish."

"You couldn't find a nice Jewish boy—or girl?" It was the first time her mother had referred to her being gay since Louey had told her years ago.

Louey laughed and hugged her mother, who patted her daughter's head. "Not for lack of trying, Ma."

"These days you have to be careful with boys, you know."

"I know, Ma."

"It's just not a good idea, Louey, with all the diseases going around."

"Next thing I know, you're going to be telling me you'd rather I was involved with a woman."

"Would that be so terrible?"

Louey's mouth dropped. Her mother: one of a kind.

By the end of the weekend, Louey had been treated to as much familial harmony as she could bear. She'd lost count of the number of times she'd been asked when she was going to get married and the number of newly divorced third cousins to whom she'd been introduced. The number of people who remembered what she did for a living, on the other hand, she could count on the fingers of one hand.

Slipping out, she took a walk until she found herself outside city limits, where on a whim she caught a bus to the town gay bar. Unlike New York bars, this one was fully mixed, male and female. She hadn't been in a gay bar anywhere for what seemed like years.

The tall woman behind the bar raised her eyebrows when she saw Louey. After filling a middle-aged man's mug, she came over. "What can I get you?" Her husky voice was the sweetest sound Louey had heard all weekend.

"What have you got?" teased Louey.

"Oh, I don't know . . ." A slow smile spread over the woman's features. "For you?"

In a little while most of the customers had left. Louey helped the bartender clear the empty glasses away and put chairs up on the tables. Then the tall woman turned to Louey with a grin.

Well! Louey thought. What was a girl to do?

When Louey got home to New York, she learned that in her absence several famous people had died of AIDS. She got into the shower, letting the water soothe her, filled with foreboding at the thought of how many of her friends she would not see grow to middle age. It was only a matter of time before someone she knew would get it, she realized. The future was laid out suddenly before her: one young man would fall, then another, and another, just as each one hit the prime of life. No wonder she never pushed dread too far from her mind.

At night she dreamed her friends were in the hospital, filling bed after bed. Tony, too frail ever to dance again, lay dressed in white, surrounded by strange people whose faces were obscured by masks. "They refuse to help me with my makeup," he complained, relaxing in her embrace like a child grateful for its mother's love. She dreamed she was walking around in heaven with people she hadn't realized had died, who showed her all the sights as if she'd arrived at a resort, a fabulous new club. Night after night she woke up in a sweat, afraid to go to sleep for fear of whom she'd find in heaven next.

One night she woke to find Clay's arms around her as

the now-familiar tears streamed from her eyes. His solid form ought to have comforted her, his body healthy as a young man's should be. Yet he seemed so far away, surreal. Kevin had just been the first to die, she thought; the rest would follow. Clay held her tightly: everyone would follow.

"Is it Kevin?" Clay asked in the morning. It seemed ridiculous to tell him she was suddenly afraid of everyone she loved dying. The rest of the world had learned to live with death. Becoming paralyzed by it amounted to a sort of insanity.

What did it mean to love someone? she wondered. Had it been a fluke that she'd loved Mia? Did she still love her? Did she love Clay, or was she merely responding to his love for her? Clay's hands tried to soothe away her sorrow. Grief brought her emotions so close to the surface, every sensation felt like pain.

One day she realized what was happening. How could she not have seen it? It was as if she were twelve years old again—yet now, instead of not being able to start crying, she couldn't stop.

For half her life, Louey had waited for catastrophe: she'd wake to find her home and family gone, she'd suddenly be penniless, abandoned. Her mother called her to a room and told her her father was dead.

As she'd grown older, some of her fear had begun to fade. Then Kevin died—and now this monstrous, inhuman disease would destroy her friends. All at once, the foundation she thought she'd established started crumbling. It was as if her father had died yesterday, only yesterday. How had she managed to put off thinking about it for so long?

How many young men would wake up to discover purple blotches on their bodies—boys who just the day before had leapt out of their beds and gone about delighting everyone who knew them? How many people would fear them, condemning them to death as if it were a punishment they deserved? How many of her friends would die, she wondered, get it and just die?

Clay told her she'd be less afraid in time. Yet all she saw was everyone she loved lined up to fall into open graves, toppling, body after body. Some nights she wished she'd never have to wake to face it.

Clay had thought love was something he knew nearly everything about, yet each day with Louey taught him something new. Sex he had thought he knew, too, yet his passion for her increased daily, when he would have expected it to fade. How could two such different people care for one another? Would she tire of him? As she dipped unfathomably toward despair, her body grew more precious, something he lived to coax joy from.

She seemed to be losing what he'd sensed in her for a long time—her resistance to the idea of him, to the notion of him as part of her future. Some days she even seemed to welcome what she felt for him. Their relationship went against everything she believed, he knew. Yet love was so rare. Surely she wouldn't turn her back on it because of the unexpected circumstances in which she'd found it? You love me, he wanted to shake her—was that so fucking terrible to admit?

It had to mean something, what they had: they loved each other. Yet as she grew more comfortable, a strange uncertainty began to gnaw at him, some odd, growing unease. At unexpected moments, his happiness would be pierced with flashes of self-doubt—but why?

One evening, to his horror, he heard himself ask her to marry him. She looked at him with astonishment and another emotion he couldn't identify. He threw himself from her apartment into the noisy comfort of the streets, trying to understand what had come over him. Marriage, for Christ's sake, he didn't even believe in marriage. It was regressing to some precognizant state even to suggest it: the ultimate slap in the face to a gay woman.

After a long walk he came back and rephrased the question: Did she want to live with him?

"I'll think about it."

Was he imagining the uneasy expression in her eyes? "No rush," he said.

"There are some things I have to tell you."

"I only need to know one thing." He cleared his throat. "Your future mailing address for tasteless postcards."

"What brought all this on?"

"Thing is," he began, "I guess I need to know what your intentions are." He tried to laugh. "I'm so conventional." She studied his face grimly. "Louey, I can't seem to stand just taking each day as it comes—is that unfair of me? Sometimes I don't have any idea what you're going to do next, if you want to—" He couldn't say it. "I have to know what you really feel for me. Is that—"

She swallowed. "It's not unfair."

He should be happy she was considering living with him, he told himself. He *was* happy. Yet a queasy panic filled him, as if the ground were suddenly crumbling under his feet.

"I'm not the only one due for some thinking," Louey pointed out. "You should take time yourself to figure out what you really want from me."

He wanted her to move in with him, that was what he wanted. Nothing could make me happier than being bound to you forever, he longed to tell her: bound. So why was part of him suddenly terrified that she might agree? What was he afraid of—what possible thing could either of them be risking—when they'd been through so much already?

She moved around the room, cleaning up without looking at him. Clay felt as if he'd jarred the serenity of their
life together, broaching some scandal that pitted them against
each other, rendered them strangers. He gathered some of
his things, looking around the apartment with a sense that
something unfathomable was happening. Slipping away: the
phrase echoed in his head. He didn't know what it could
be, but he was losing something irretrievable. Giving her a
kiss, he left, closing the door behind him. The soft click
echoed in his ears as if it were the discharge of a pistol.

Louey awoke to a discovery: she loved him. Could that be possible? She lay in bed, studying the ceiling as the words reverberated through her head. It was true; she loved him. It astonished her. Who would have thought her simple pleasure in his company could unexpectedly turn into something deeper? A feeling of calm seeped through her. How had something like this happened without her even noticing? Typical, she thought, when life outside convention gave her such delight, her sly emotions tricked her into this collaboration.

She picked up the phone, hanging up before she'd made the connection. What would she have said: I love you, isn't that a riot? He would hardly have been amused. She shook herself, sighing, and got up to go to work.

In the middle of the afternoon the thought came into her head: never to make love with a woman again. She stared at lines of text in front of her, unable to focus. How could she bear it? Never to kiss a woman. How could she give that up forever? You're the one who feels sorry for anyone who isn't gay, she told herself, remember? She hadn't realized what she would be giving up if she stayed with Clay.

If she told him about sleeping with the woman back home, he would probably leave her. How *could* she love him?

But she did love him. It was ridiculous, but she did. Jesus: was she actually contemplating moving in with a man? It was too alien a notion to consider seriously. What was it she had with him; could it be anything like what she'd had with Mia? She didn't *want* anything like that with a man. Her own mother, with all her wishes for an easy life, would not expect that of her. But Clay wasn't "a man": he was just Clay. What was so terrible about loving him?

To keep his mind off the future, Clay dredged up his old manuscript. It was both better than he'd remembered and more fundamentally flawed than he'd expected. How on earth could he write a book if he couldn't even think of how to end it? What was love, anyway? What made him feel so lost thinking about it? He was just unaccustomed to being alone, he told himself; Louey was such a basic component of his life he couldn't function properly without her.

The faceless uncertainty continued to gnaw at him. What could he be so worried about? She would either say yes or no, and if no, that didn't mean she was going to walk out of his life forever. And if she said yes? Wasn't that what he'd dreamt of—proof she loved him so much she was willing to do something absolutely out of character?

He didn't want her to be out of character, that was the problem. As he thought of her compromising, he envisioned Louey changing, trapped, like so many people dimmed by the details of ordinary life. Would she become less and less the woman he loved, the more she changed for him? How fair was it to ask her?

He wanted to live with her, couldn't imagine not being with her. Yet what if years went by and one day she awoke and realized she'd betrayed all she was, all she cared about? Would she blame him, then, for what he'd done to her? Would she grow to despise herself— and him?

It made no sense, thought Louey. If she refused to love someone simply because he was a man, how was that any different from the world denying her the right to love a woman? What was the big deal, living with him, anyway? She wouldn't lose her life; it wouldn't change what she felt about anything. Being with one person always meant giving up what you might have with anyone else. Everyone in relationships made the same concession. And if she found that she couldn't be happy with him—because he wasn't a woman, for whatever reason—she'd stop seeing him. No relationship was guaranteed to be permanent; she'd known few that were. What she had with Clay was bound to change eventually. She was gay, for Christ's sake. Then why live with him? she wondered.

On the other hand, since she loved him, why not?

By the end of the week Clay had hardly slept a night, stalking the city for hours like a homeless man. One night, when he lay down, something in him gave. Never again could he let anything, any one person, put him in this state. Life could never rise and fall on circumstances he could not control; that way lay madness.

The night before he was to meet Louey, he came home to find a message from her on his machine: she would meet him at a certain restaurant at eight (she would be the one with teeth). He turned the machine off, running a hand through his hair. Instinctively he moved to fix himself a drink. She sounded cheerful, which meant the news was good, or so he had to hope. Catching sight of his face in the hall mirror on the way to depositing his jacket, he lifted his glass in a toast.

"Here's to your future, baby," he said. Soon enough he'd hear the verdict, good or bad. It shouldn't really matter what it was.

Why was it he felt like crying?

After thirty-five minutes, the maître d' came over to Clay to say Miss Mercer had called to tell him she was going to be late. He had been surprised at the butterflies that overtook him as he sat waiting; why he should be so anxious he couldn't imagine. Reason told him that she was late due to something minor, yet he couldn't help feeling a purely irrational sense of foreboding. What if she didn't come at all? What if she had realized she was making the biggest mistake of her life? Why hadn't he been satisfied to leave things as they were—marriage, for God's sake, where had that idea come from? It was all this misery that had overtaken her recently; it had made him want to pledge himself to her, to glue her to him.

This was craziness. She would be here. He was insane to worry—he wouldn't ruin her just by living with her, she was sleeping with him as it was, for Christ's sake, and she hadn't been contaminated with normality, had she?

The waiters and other customers looked at him with alternating pity and curiosity, as if he were dolled up for a blind date who was obviously jilting him. After an hour, the gnawing in his stomach got the better of him and he called her apartment. The phone rang and rang. He called his machine to see if she'd left him a message, but there was no word. He went back to his table, determined to renew his vigil, but his trip to the phone had somehow killed his desire to stay, and he paid the check, leaving a message with the waiter in case Louey came after he'd gone. The last thing he was going to do was sit and wait as if eagerly anticipating bad news.

He had to do something. She'd been murdered on the street, on the subway; she'd been kidnapped, pushed under a train. He would never forgive himself if something had happened to her. With a growing sense of dread, Clay made his way to her apartment.

Louey had been zipping up her dress when a knock came on her door. Silly boy, she thought, opening it with a flourish.

"May I come in?"

Louey took a step back. Mia stood in her doorway, her hair in disarray around her face.

"I know I should have called," Mia was saying. Louey moved back and they were both inside before she knew how it had happened. The room seemed tiny, cramped. "You probably would have hung up on me."

"I can't talk to you," Louey blurted.

Mia stared. Louey felt the outline of her body wavering, as if she were dissolving into tiny particles. How could Mia be here? Mia said something about the party (Party? Louey thought), then on the street, why wouldn't Louey talk to her? There seemed to be an echo. ". . . do I have to do?" said Mia, do? voice faltering, just tell me what I have to do.

Louey groped for a nearby chair, sinking into it. "You stopped," she stuttered. "Everything just stopped."

"You know I never stopped loving you." Had Mia really said that? It seemed cruelly surreal. "Does this mean all a person has to do is make one mistake . . . someone you love . . ." (Louey's head was throbbing) ". . . another chance?" Louey covered her face.

"Are you all right?" Mia knelt, a hand on Louey's knee, the other reaching to her cheek. Louey wrenched herself away, head spinning, bolted to the bathroom, splashing water on her face, the small room closing in on her, face in the mirror wild-eyed, unfamiliar. How could Mia be here, now?

The sight that greeted Louey on returning to the living room nearly made her stagger, reaching for the wall. Mia was crumpled on the floor, collapsed, face in her hands: Mia was crying. Never had she seen Mia like this, defeated; it was wrenching. Louey stumbled for the phone, leaving a message, her eyes frozen on the sight of Mia: Mia helpless and distraught was the only possibility she'd never considered, the only problem she was powerless to solve. Kneeling, she put her arms on Mia's shoulders. "Don't. *Please*, Mia."

"I waited," Mia said, "until I had the nerve." Her voice pierced right through Louey. "Till I was sure he was gone."

"He?"

"Yes"—suddenly defiant—"I saw you with him, but then for a while he didn't come, so then I . . ." Waited to make sure, Mia was saying; some strange roaring built in Louey's ears. ". . . courage to face you." Mia, building courage?

"So does this mean once someone hurts you," Mia said again, "they never get another chance?" Her voice seemed far away; surely it was someone other than Mia who'd been watching her apartment until Clay was really gone? ". . . what it took to force myself to knock." Louey swallowed: forced herself? "I never knew what I was doing," Mia cried out. "Don't you realize that? You always thought I had all the answers—Christ, I didn't have a clue. What the fuck has someone like *me* got to offer?"

"Timeless beauty?" Louey tried to tease her.

"What good is that if you don't want me?" Mia flung herself against Louey, muffled: "I know I was a bitch"—eyes glistening—"bitch goddess."

Louey closed her eyes. This was a mirage, she knew. It would disappear, her life would go on as planned—but how? She had no life. Was what Mia had asked her true: was she incapable of forgiving someone she had loved? Mia's hands clutched at her shoulders, waist, tears streaming from her eyes, excruciating. "Mia—" She twisted her head away. "I don't know what to tell you—" Mia pressed her mouth to Louey's; Louey tasted tears. "I don't—"

"It's no good without you."

"Mia . . ." Mia's head against her shoulder felt like anguish piercing through her. "You have to make it be good," she murmured, stroking Mia's hair. Fine advice, she thought, coming from her. How could she have convinced herself she could make any life-and-death decision? "Make it be good yourself." How could she tell Mia to let go when she could barely get herself to do so? "That shouldn't be too hard for a bitch goddess like you."

Mia tried to smile. Amazing: who would have believed Mia could look like that?

What was she supposed to do?

By the time Clay reached Louey's apartment, it beckoned like an old friend. You are ludicrously over-dressed, he thought; he never should have started this whole business. Maybe she was late because she'd cooked up some surprise for him which taxed her organizational skills more than she'd expected. He wouldn't even be upset, as long as she was fine—alive. Climbing her stairs, he couldn't help but feel his usual anticipation at the thought of seeing her. "Take off those clothes," she'd say; what good were clothes for what was truly meaningful in life?

"Louey?" he called, knocking on the door. Silence. He tried the knob; to his considerable unease, it turned in his hand. He went inside.

The first sight that greeted him was the dress he'd bought, draped over a chair. He called Louey's name again, the hair on the back of his neck prickling at the prospect of a prolonged evening of mystery. Surely if anything serious had really happened to her, she wouldn't have called the restaurant? He dialed the number, then hung up, his stomach sinking when the maître d' told him she had never shown up or called again. And you were worried about

246

scarring her psyche, he thought; she would love the irony in that.

When he discovered what was waiting in the bedroom, however, he lost all desire to see the irony in anything.

The bed was stripped; the dresser and the closet both were open, scavenged as completely as if someone had ransacked them and then fled. Numbly Clay thought of the dress still waiting in the other room: a thief would not have taken jeans and underwear and left a high-priced evening gown. He almost wished it was a thief who'd done this.

Mocked by the empty hangers, he closed the closet gently, slid the dresser drawers back so that the piece looked seemly once again. He lost heart looking at the bed and sank onto it, wondering what possible use for bedclothes even a desperately deranged Louey could have.

Staring at his bewildered reflection in the mirror, he caught sight of a piece of paper beside him on the pillow. He turned, his heart thudding. Ransom note? he thought, though it was not the worst possibility that occurred to him. Then, after reading what it said, he lay back on the bare mattress and covered his face with shaking hands.

"Wine?"

Clay shook his head, thanking the young woman hovering before him. He couldn't believe this was happening: all around him were copies of his book, people he'd never met were clapping him on the back. Young women in black bow ties offered him drinks, hors d'oeuvres and knowing smiles, as if he were truly important and not (he imagined her wry voice) merely pretty.

Well, he'd finished it. He'd found himself a publisher, a nice young editor as honest as he was hardworking—no mean feat, as Clay had learned from Louey. It wasn't this poor young man's fault he was no Louey, Clay thought. ("Thank God for small favors," he imagined her telling him.) He felt a twinge of sadness that she wasn't here for this, she who had been so much a part of it.

When she'd left him, he had tried to drink himself into amnesia, but it hadn't worked. How could agony like this not kill him? Everywhere he went, he looked for her; every day, he waited for her call. How could she have done this to him? He hated himself for wanting her so much; he hated her for making him want her. He hated the smug, insular world of women who needed only each other. Why had he imagined she could ever care about him?

"Come on," he whispered late at night, his body aching. "It's not funny anymore."

Still, after months had passed, he started thinking more dispassionately: this must be what she'd been going through with Mia, he realized. And even as she'd longed for Mia, she had come to love him—him. That was no small thing, was it? Who would have believed that he could love someone so different from himself, so far from what he'd always thought he'd end up with, and that she could love him, too? Somehow she had made him realize there was more to him than he had thought, and more to life.

When he thought of what she'd given him—he who hadn't had any right to expect anything from her—he lost all will to hate her, to begrudge her happiness with someone she still loved. One thing she'd taught him was to let go of useless longing, to be happy for whatever someone else could give you, and not dwell on what they couldn't give. At least she'd never gotten tired of him—not that she ever would have, he thought huffily.

Whether he could see her and still feel such noble sentiments, of course, was not quite as clear. Yet when the book became an actual living thing (he was surprised at how he thought of it—another thing he'd picked up from her), he couldn't help but try to find her.

The operator had no listing for her, and her old number now seemed to belong to someone with a heavy Rumanian accent. Her office said she'd taken a leave of absence to do freelance work but wouldn't tell him where she'd gone. Short of putting an ad in the newspaper or pasting signs all over New York, it seemed he had no way of finding her.

His agent jostled his arm, smiling at him—everyone was smiling, as if he'd suddenly done something, accomplished something miraculous. If only she were here, the only person whose approval would mean anything; he ached to see her smile at him. Wherever she was, he hoped she was all right—happy. He hoped she was happy.

The drinks flowed and chatter enveloped him like an embrace. His friends and so many people who had worked to help him—even some of his family—all were here to celebrate in these lovely rooms above a bookstore. It amazed him: people gave so freely of themselves for something they needn't consider for an instant. "Wait till your *next* book," they said, as if he could write without her help. (Now, now, he told himself: no more of that.)

He had tried to write about her, but his attempts to call forth her silly glee rang false. The passages he wrote about her pain brought him up short—how strange to draw forth tears from the hand you wrote with!—but he could barely read them by the light of day.

Some of her friends had shown up, no doubt as surprised by his invitations as he'd been to send them. They seemed to brighten up the room, glimmers of cheer among the earnest faces.

Looking around the animated crowd, he imagined he saw Louey, teasing someone playfully; she would glance up, catch him watching her and wink. The thought was painful. He couldn't stand another minute in this room, he realized; he could hardly bear another second in a building full of people who weren't Louey. Thanking as many people as he could, he turned and fled. As he hurried down the stairs, it seemed to him that he could hear her laughter float above the others' in the room.

"Let's spend lots of money," Mia said. "God, let's go do something crazy."

Louey looked at the calendar and counted off the time: three, four, five months and six days. They'd had less than half a year; she could never go back.

"What are you waiting for?" asked Mia.

She wouldn't say she never should have; it had shown her something: what the past had meant and how much she had changed. Crazy? she thought. Why? What had once seemed daring now seemed somehow pointless; wildness meant so little without something like joy to fuel it.

"You seem—different," Mia said.

She was different—someone else entirely. She'd been luckier than most people alive to have had a love like Mia once. But she could never be a girl again.

Closing the closet, she finished packing the clothes into her suitcase. She had moved in and out of so many sublets over the past year that she'd become expert at packing all her possessions in less than an hour. The feeling of rootlessness and despair that had begun to overtake her the last few times had mellowed into a kind of carefree adventuresomeness. If she wanted to, she realized, she could pick up and go live in any city in the world. Freelance work had proven plentiful, despite the cautionary tales she had encountered when she'd talked about quitting. She had even started to find solitude enjoyable.

Life with Mia had been heaven on earth the first time around—for longer than she'd had any right to expect. The light had blinded whenever Mia came into a room; all life had drained away once she had left it. The second time around, though, everything was different. "What's the matter?" Mia would ask—but Louey didn't know how to explain why she could no longer be the blissful playmate Mia wanted, or why the world they'd lived in, that enchanted island, seemed to have vanished forever.

"All I want is to be happy," she tried to explain: to love her work, hear music, and love Mia. Yet though the bodies still worked perfectly, the hearts were now somehow too far apart to bridge the past. She had learned something by loving Clay: other things mattered as much as bodies. Truly being happy with another person meant being utterly and happily yourself, not turning into someone else. You traveled through the world alone, and if somebody gave you love and you could give it back, if you drew forth someone's best self and she drew yours, it was miraculous. Yet ultimately, being happy was in your hands alone. Whatever anyone else could give you was pure bonus.

She'd lost Mia. Mia, who still took pleasure throwing everyone off balance, was now, herself, undone. Louey loved her, but it wasn't any use; it only left her wanting something else. Mia skimmed the surfaces of life, afraid to go too deep; the things that lay beneath frightened her too much to test. Louey had seen a glimpse of what Mia feared: a father married to someone who grew more and more aloof the more he worshipped her. Once Mia had tried to explain why she had left: how she'd come home one day to find Louey so absorbed in her work she hadn't even noticed

Mia's presence. "The walls closed in on me," said Mia. "It took every last drop of strength I had just to turn and walk out of the room." But Mia didn't seem to understand that everyone was not her parents; real love didn't have to overwhelm, or turn into contempt.

Louey wasn't certain why Mia had loved her, why Clay wanted her. She'd never given Clay all he'd hoped for, though she'd given all she could. She hated herself for hurting him, but she could never have been the woman he wanted; no doubt it would have ended badly if she'd tried.

What was it that made people love each other? Would she ever know?

She could close her eyes and still recall the time she'd first made love with Mia, and with Clay. The memories were as clear as if the first times had been only yesterday. Now she would also remember the last.

It was the middle of a warm summer day when Clay walked down a narrow London street, turned a corner, and came face to face with Mia D'Allesandro. "Look at this," she said, as if he were a scientific oddity she was pointing out to someone other than himself. Numb with surprise, Clay started to move past her, but she shifted the packages in her arms, putting out a hand to stop him. "Don't you dare. I'll never live it down if you don't come with me."

"What might you be doing here, Mia?" he asked as casually as he could manage. She steered him to a bench in one of the multitude of small parks that graced London, this one opposite a row of greengrocers and small stores.

"We flew in to see a show," Mia replied, "just for the weekend." She seemed distracted, and he followed her wandering eyes to a store filled with women shopping for their families. "Oh, wait, I've got something to show you," she added, fussing with her packages until she produced a book from a small brown paper bag. "You've got to inscribe it for Louey." She handed him the British edition of his novel. Seeing his surprise, she explained, "She just bought it for me, but I'll get another one back home." He frowned; why buy the book while they were traveling, instead of just going to their neighborhood store—wherever their neighborhood was? "Come on, you have to write something, it'll mean so much to her." Mia cracked open the book. "Here, near the tacky dedication." He looked at her for a moment, then had to laugh. She smiled, an actual smile, and handed him the book.

"What do you think"—he searched for a pen—"witty or sincere?"

"I think you've already covered sincere." She pointed to the printed dedication.

He read it: To Louisa Mercer, for a gift I can never repay. "Maybe you're right." He smiled, putting pen to paper and considering. Quickly he wrote a few words, closed the book and turned to face her. "Anything else?"

"I understand it's not too bad," she said, "all things considered. She loved the ending, by the way." Clay stared at her, confused to feel grateful for any words from Mia's lips. Could he really be sitting on a bench in London with this woman, waiting for Louey? He felt nervous hysteria well up in him.

When Louey found them, they were both laughing so hard the tears were streaming down their cheeks. "Well," she drawled, "this is a pretty picture." She came and put her packages down, shaking her head. "The last face on earth." She hugged Clay quickly. "I was wondering when I'd run into you."

"I just *got* here." He wasn't sure if he was stunned or delighted, but Louey didn't seem surprised to see him. "What show did you see?"

"What? Oh, I didn't come for the show. I live here." She laughed at his expression. He drank in the sight of her, all glowing eyes and skin. "Mia and Sally came to see the latest Andrew Lloyd Webber."

"Sally?"

"Yeah, Sally," Mia interjected. "Which reminds me, I have a plane to catch and we aren't even packed. Baby"—she put her arms around Louey—"thanks for everything. We had a great time. See you—?"

"November, I think." Louey kissed her, making Clay feel strangely avuncular.

"You," Mia told Clay, "I'm sure I'll run into again." She held her hand out and he took it (she had a firm handshake, naturally). "Bye." She glanced again at Louey, then abruptly left them alone.

"Sally?"

Louey turned to him. "You guys rehearse this?"

" 'Sally'?"

"Sally"—Louey took one of his hands—"is Mia's new girlfriend." Seeing his expression, she smiled sadly. "You know how it is—once you break a heart, it never quite works the same again."

"I know how it is," he said. Her smile faded. "Please tell me she didn't break your heart again."

"No. This time, you'll be happy to know, I was the one who left her." She cleared her throat. "We won't dwell on the fact that Sally looks suspiciously like me, however, since we both know it was the inner woman she loved."

"I'll *bet*."

"I cannot believe Mia ran into you." He took her hand. "Oh, but—Clay, the book is wonderful. I loved the ending."

"So I hear." He proffered the copy Mia had made him inscribe, and she flushed, reading his words.

"Thank you," she said softly, not looking up.

"So you missed the British publication of my book," he teased.

"Who do you think sent those purple tulips to your hotel?" He stared at her. "Or are there so many possibilities you can't keep track?"

"Louey. I never—" He covered his face. "When I first

saw them, I thought of every—I thought it was a cruel joke, some sick twist of fate."

"Fate?" She shook her head. "Not even Fate would dare torment a boy like you." She grimaced. "I'm the only one who does that kind of thing."

He didn't answer.

"So have you—" She couldn't bring herself to say it. "Do you—?"

"Nothing to forgive," he said. It startled him that it was true.

"I see we have a difference of opinion. Perhaps you'd like me to jog your memory."

"I won't pretend I wouldn't have hoped for things to work out differently."

She fastened shining eyes on his.

"You could at least have left me the children," he added.

Her smile was tremulous.

"Louey," he blurted, "it wasn't your fault what happened, not with Mia or with me. I wish you hadn't gone the way you did"—she looked down—"and there's no point denying I would rather you had loved me—loved me more." He put a hand up, stopping her. "For about half a year I hated you. I did. But then I realized I'd expected you to give up everything for me." He paused. "Of course you blamed yourself for all of it, right? *Someone* had to leap to your defense."

She kept her eyes fastened on her feet, blinking back tears.

"No, of course you're right," he went on. "I never should have let you—*touch* me, for God's sake." He shuddered. "Once that happened, you got so pushy, I—well, I don't know how I put up with it."

"It was wonderful," she said. He waited for her to look up and smile. Instead, she opened his book and read the dedication. "You're wrong, you know. You've more than repaid me."

"You mean the mink, the diamonds, the Mercedes?" He waved a hand. "Keep 'em."

A woman passed them, eyeing Louey; the two smiled at each other, then quickly looked away. Louey stole a glance at him, blushing. "Anyone we know?" he teased.

"You might say that." She blushed again. "Clay—" She grabbed his arm. "I nearly cried the day I found your book in the stores—and I *did* cry when I opened it." She put her hand on his knee. "It's magical." He flushed with pleasure. "I was wondering how you were going to end it."

She flipped to the back of the book and read: *And when they'd been sitting together for several hours, he at the piano, she reading on his couch, he realized that the simple fact of having her there, his friend, made him happy. He'd felt none of the jealousy or sweeping moods with her that he did with the women he'd thought he loved; she was only his best friend, whose affection he had never doubted, whom he trusted implicitly. As he turned to face her, something of his surprise must have shown on his face, for she laughed and asked what great truth he'd just stumbled upon.*

"That you make me happy and that you're my best friend in the world."

"What a relief; the tumor must have dissolved," she said, returning to her book. He rose from the piano and sat next to her, feeling he would burst from the urgency of what he had to convince her. "Yes?" she asked indulgently, not looking up.

"Do you love me?"

"Isn't that what you pay me for?" She closed her book. "What's the matter? Had another fight with your latest boopsie?"

"How about going away with me somewhere for the weekend?" he said, impatient. She didn't have the slightest clue.

"What has gotten into you?" She poked him in the stomach. "Has that vixen gotten you in trouble?" He took her hand and she frowned, puzzled by his earnestness.

How had he thought he could find with some woman whose appearance intoxicated him what he'd had all along with the woman sitting on his couch? He couldn't believe he'd nearly passed up love merely because they had taken the trouble to win each other's loyalty and friendship and never once considered romance. Love wasn't the heady attraction of chemistry but a bond tested over time and deepened by the terrors of living and changing, sharing pain and silly trifling pleasures.

She called him her little pal but she would always be there when he needed her; if that wasn't love, what was? Well, perhaps theirs was too familiar a bond to encourage passion; they would find that out soon enough. Yet when she studied his face, he thought he'd burst from wanting her.

"What is going on in that tiny head of yours?" she said fondly, and he couldn't stand the suspense, pulling her to him fiercely and kissing her. She started, only to relax in his arms and return his kiss as naturally as if they'd been doing this all along. This was so different from everything he'd known, this was something that was going to make him delirious with happiness. Finally he let her go, looking at a face so familiar he was surprised to see it was the same face he'd known before he'd kissed it.

"Feel better now?" she asked. "Or is there more silliness you need to get out of your system?"

"More." He took her hand, raising her to her feet. "Much more silliness. Sorry. Won't take but a decade of your time."

"We'll see about that." She laughed, and put her arms around him.

Louey closed the book.

"Wishful thinking." He smiled, rueful.

"Nobody's perfect." She smiled back, patting the cover of the book. "And you?" she asked. "Found a new one yet?"

He listened to her own unspoken answer, the calm resolution in her voice reverberating as she waited to hear about his life. Why did he feel, sitting here with her, as if no time had passed? "Was it wrong of me to want you?"

"I thought so." She regarded him so tenderly he couldn't feel offended. "At the time I thought if I loved you I was betraying everything I cared about."

"And weren't you?"

"How could it be a betrayal to love someone? That's what we're for." She touched his arm. "Nothing's that black-and-white. You don't turn into a completely different person just because you love a boy—a homely, dull-witted boy."

He felt a flush of pleasure. "I see a certain logic in your thinking," he mentioned shyly.

"So what is your agenda here in London?"

He studied her face. For no reason, his heart was hammering; he concentrated all his energies on slowing it to normal. "Rest and relaxation," he said. "Got to store up all I can to work on my next book." He grinned. "Can't have them saying I'm some one-shot flavor of the month."

"And how are your accommodations?"

The smile she gave him was so lewd he had to laugh. "Adequate," he said, "though not nearly as luxurious as yours, I'm sure."

"No?" She brushed the hair from his face.

"So." He swallowed, clearing his throat. "What's happening in November?"

"I'm coming to New York." She lowered her eyes. "I'm trying to put together a show of paintings, and I think I'll be ready by then."

"Paintings?" he said, mouth agape. "Yours?"

She grinned unabashedly, as if she'd been caught doing something embarrassingly childish. "I know. Who would have figured it?"

"*Louey.*"

"Yeah." She blushed, shrugging.

He stared.

"So"—she faltered—"do you think . . ." She raised her eyes to his. "While you're here, uh, would you like to—"

It occurred to Clay that nothing would be simpler than taking her in his arms. If there were some weakness in such a desire, he couldn't see it. "What if someone more homely and dull-witted comes along?"

"Hell"—she shrugged—"let 'em join us. More the merrier." She began giggling. "Hey, *I'm* open-minded." He started to exclaim, but before he knew it she had reached up and kissed him, her lips lingering. "I *love* you," she said, as if it were so obvious it was a wonder she had to say it. "I'll get over it, of course," she added, smiling.

Startled, he laughed. "You"—he shook a finger at her—"are a tawdry human being. In fact, I don't think I care to stand for another minute of such—"

She put a hand over his mouth, then drew an arm around him, pressing a warm cheek to his. "You only live once," she whispered, her eyes shimmering. She lay her head on his shoulder, not quite over his heart.